MORE PRAISE FOR

*SHE OF THE MOUNTAINS:*
WITHDRAWN

*She of the Mountains* is a wonderfully textured book that knows better than to offer hasty answers about identity—rather Shraya draws us into a series of highly poetic and hyper-intimate scenes that allows us to feel and explore for ourselves.

—Amber Dawn, AUTHOR OF
*Sub Rosa* AND *How Poetry Saved My Life*

*She of the Mountains* is a forthright, honest, damned sexy book written, gleefully and counter-intuitively, in a lyrical, epic, transcendent style. It is not your typical debut novel, but rather one ripped apart at the spine and then reconfigured via alchemy, Tantric mysticism, the open verse of social media, and pure, raw talent. Sensual, smart (and smart-assed), *She of the Mountains* is the beginning of something big, bold, and—hold your purse!—glamorous.

—R.M. Vaughan, AUTHOR OF *Compared to Hitler*

Given the intersection of Vivek Shraya's writing and his music up till now, it should come as no surprise that his newest book is an equally compelling fusion of stories, voices, and textures. *She of the Mountains* is a touching and transporting prose-poem that has a music all its own.

—Rakesh Satyal, AUTHOR OF *Blue Boy*

D0188483

# SHE

*of the*

# MOUNTAINS

## VIVEK SHRAYA

**Arsenal Pulp Press**

*Vancouver*

SHE OF THE MOUNTAINS
Copyright © 2014 by Vivek Shraya

All rights reserved. No part of this book may be reproduced in any part by any means—graphic, electronic, or mechanical—without the prior written permission of the publisher, except by a reviewer, who may use brief excerpts in a review, or in the case of photocopying in Canada, a license from Access Copyright.

ARSENAL PULP PRESS
Suite 202–211 East Georgia St.
Vancouver, BC V6A 1Z6
Canada
*arsenalpulp.com*

The publisher gratefully acknowledges the support of the Canada Council for the Arts and the British Columbia Arts Council for its publishing program, and the Government of Canada (through the Canada Book Fund) and the Government of British Columbia (through the Book Publishing Tax Credit Program) for its publishing activities.

This is a work of fiction. Any resemblance of characters to persons either living or deceased is purely coincidental.

Illustrations (including cover) by Raymond Biesinger
Design by Gerilee McBride
Edited by Susan Safyan
Author photograph © Zachary Ayotte

Printed and bound in Canada

Library and Archives Canada Cataloguing in Publication:

Shraya, Vivek, 1981–, author
         She of the mountains / Vivek Shraya.

Issued in print and electronic formats.
ISBN 978-1-55152-560-0 (pbk.).—ISBN 978-1-55152-561-7 (epub)

         I. Title.

PS8637.H73S54 2014          C813'.6          C2014-903727-9
                                                        C2014-903728-7

*To Shemeena*

In the beginning, there is no he. There is no she.

Two cells make up one cell. This is the mathematics behind creation. One plus one makes one. Life begets life. We are the period to a sentence, the effect to a cause, always belonging to someone. We are never our own.

This is why we are so lonely.

Briefly, ever so briefly, we linger as one. Our true first. Then we divide over and over again, always by two.

Inside the body of another, our heart is constructed. Inside the body of another, our heart drums its first beat.

Other organs form too. Skin stretches, bones harden, teeth bud. Sound is captured. Light is perceived.

If given the choice, we would stay here forever, sleeping. Pure and golden potential. But outside, they wait for us, sing to us, name us. They sculpt expectations we will not live up to, imagine medals we will not win, dream of highways we will not build, and hope for reformations we will not make.

Pushed out of the body of another, in sweat and screams, we experience the greatest rejection we will ever know. Out of warm fluid and into rough, biting air. No coo or pat or praise can ever compensate for this violence.

This is why we are so lonely.

PARVATI

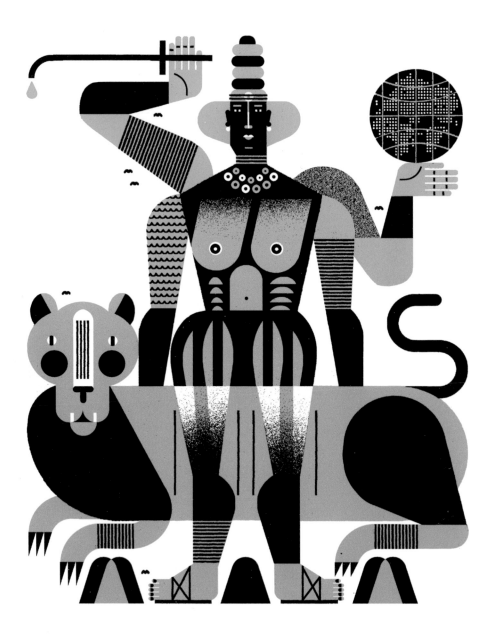

I am the mother of the universe.

I am the planets and the years of darkness and light in between.

I am the oceans, the sky, the land, the air—the four corners.

I am life itself, the spark that makes a heart pump, that keeps a tree alive for centuries, green and reaching.

I am Parvati.

Today, I need a shower. Life can be filthy.

I apply a paste made of crushed sandalwood and jasmine to my skin with a circular motion. Right-hand fingers slowly spread over left hand, over left wrist, around left elbow, up left arm, over left shoulder.

I sing, but no one can hear me. The notes are too high, the melody too beautiful. Not even my husband can hear me—not just because he is out hunting right now. Shiv, my beloved Shiv, is often buried deep within his own mind, seduced by the possibility of an even quieter silence, a firmer stillness, the kind that borders death. Sometimes I think he has more in common with the corpses in that graveyard he has been dancing in lately than he does with me.

The First Song was born from pure grief. It happened the instant I felt the heartbeat of the first life form, my first child, stop. I was at the foot of our mountain Kailash when my mouth opened in pain, and the first notes, too high to be a scream, too beautiful to be a howl, ran up from my diaphragm through my throat and into the dawn. Being married to Shiv, Lord of Destruction, I understood the necessity of death, but this did not make my loss any easier to endure. Days passed in song and mourning, and I vowed never to create life again.

But is there anything more consoling, more exhilarating, than creation itself?

I look down at my body, covered in brown paste that lightens as it hardens, and wait patiently. When the paste is firm and tan, I gently peel it off, this time starting at my right toe, over right ankle, up right calf, over right knee, up right leg. I sing a different song, my voice cascading like desert sands, each peak unique and transient. The tiny hairs along the newly exposed skin respond to my voice, standing at full attention. But it's not just my own body that responds.

I notice that the crumbled paste in my hands is softening to my song, turning golden. Excited, I continue singing and removing the paste from my body, adding it to the other remnants in my hand. My song gets clearer and faster, the flow of air in my throat running effortlessly back and forth over the scale, stopping briefly at the mid-notes, creating the sound of wind gliding over rivers and eroding stone.

I am naked now. All the paste has been removed and formed into a radiant ball of clay that vibrates with the sound of my voice. My hands take over: they pull, ply, roll, mould, and stretch the clay.

I know what's happening in my hands. I know this feeling so well, but every time, I weep. With every sprout of grass, every bursting new star, I weep.

When I clear the water from my eyes, I see that I am standing face to face with a statue of a young boy. With my final note, he opens his eyes.

Without hesitation, I pull him into my arms and say: Your name is Ganesha. Ganesha, my son.

He says nothing, but I know he can hear me, his eyelids fluttering. I tell Ganesha to guard our home while I rinse off.

*Let no one in. Under any circumstance.*

It is not protection I seek, but a moment for myself, a moment undisturbed by the prayers and plights of my children. As I finish the final part of my cleanse, rinsing the oil and salt of creation off my body, I can't help but sing as I think of my new son. For a moment, I think I can even hear him humming along in the distance, and again I cry.

When I emerge, I find Ganesha's head on the doorstep, next to his headless body.

• • •

The first time she put her hand on his body, he winced.

And the second time.

The third time, he cried.

The fifty-seventh time.

Then, gradually, he began to lose count. He relaxed. Her touch was still painful, but now, instead of fearing it, fearing what her hands might discover, the ugly they might find, the coarseness of a terrain unclaimed or untravelled, he anticipated it. He desired it.

After years of hiding and being unseen, her touch was a deep thawing, a memory of heat lost long ago.

• • •

*GO!*

He waited for the boys to push past him before he picked up his feet and trailed behind with a slow, contented jog. Every so often, when one of the boys passed him on their fourth or fifth round of the track, he would catch a whiff of their sweat and competitive spirit. He recalled what his mother had said about his long legs being destined for greatness as his body picked up speed. For a short distance, with every thrust forward and every leap into the air, he felt boundless, weightless. Looking up at the sky instead of straight ahead, he briefly mirrored its vast possibility. A shortage of air soon deflated his flight back to a jog. Panting, he reminded himself that the exhilaration he had momentarily experienced was what mattered.

This logic was wrong and was corrected with two words. *You're gay*, the other boys said when he finished the race last.

At first, he was certain that they could have used any two words. The assault was in the repetition:

*you're gay, you're gay! YOU're gay, you're gay, you're gay, you're GAY, you're gay, you're gay, you're GAY, you're gay! you're gay, you're gay! you're GAY, You're Gay, you're gay, you're gay, YOU're gay, you're gay, you're Gay, you're gay, you're gay, YOU're gay, you're gay! you're gay, You're Gay, you're GAY, you're gay. you're gay, you're gay! YOU're gay, you're gay, you're gay, you're GAY, you're gay, you're gay, you're GAY, you're gay! you're gay, you're gay! you're GAY, You're Gay, you're gay, you're gay, YOU're gay, you're gay, you're Gay, you're gay, you're gay, YOU're gay, you're*

*gay! you're gay, You're Gay, you're GAY, you're gay. you're gay,*
*you're gay! YOU're gay, you're gay, you're gay, you're GAY, you're*
*gay, you're gay, you're GAY, you're gay! you're gay, you're gay! you're*
*GAY, You're Gay, you're gay, you're gay, YOU're gay, you're gay,*
*you're Gay, you're gay, you're gay, YOU're gay, you're gay! you're*
*gay, You're Gay, you're GAY, you're gay. you're gay, you're gay!*
*YOU're gay, you're gay, you're gay, you're GAY, you're gay, you're*
*gay, you're GAY, you're gay! you're gay, you're gay! you're GAY,*
*You're Gay, you're gay, you're gay, YOU're gay, you're gay, you're*
*Gay, you're gay, you're gay, YOU're gay, you're gay! you're gay,*
*You're Gay, you're GAY, you're gay. you're gay, you're gay! YOU're*
*gay, you're gay, you're gay, you're GAY, you're gay, you're gay,*
*you're GAY, you're gay! you're gay, you're gay! you're GAY, You're*
*Gay, you're gay, you're gay, YOU're gay, you're gay, you're Gay,*
*you're gay, you're gay, YOU're gay, you're gay! you're gay, You're*
*Gay, you're GAY, you're gay. you're gay, you're gay! YOU're gay,*
*you're gay, you're gay, you're GAY, you're gay, you're gay, you're*
*GAY, you're gay! you're gay, you're gay! you're GAY, You're Gay,*
*you're gay, you're gay, YOU're gay, you're gay, you're Gay, you're*
*gay, you're gay, you're gay! YOU're gay, you're gay, you're gay,*
*you're GAY, you're gay, you're gay, you're GAY, you're gay! you're*
*gay, you're gay! YOU're gay, you're gay, you're gay, you're GAY,*
*you're gay, you're gay, you're GAY, you're gay! you're gay, you're*
*gay! YOU're gay, you're gay, you're gay, you're GAY, you're gay,*
*you're gay, you're GAY, you're gay! you're gay, you're gay! YOU're*
*gay, you're gay, you're gay, you're GAY, you're gay, you're gay,*
*you're GAY, you're gay! you're gay, you're gay! YOU're gay, you're*
*gay, you're gay, you're GAY, you're gay, you're gay, you're GAY,*
*you're gay! you're gay, you're gay! YOU're gay, you're gay, you're*
*gay, you're GAY, you're gay, you're gay, you're GAY, you're gay!*

*You're gay* became a virus that spread beyond gym class, past the mouths of boys who seemed to be jealous of his friendships with the prettiest girls in the school. The replication forced him to wonder what it was about the particular sounds that constructed such a small word—*GG-AE-EY*—that was so contagious.

One afternoon, he strode swiftly to the back of the library where the giant school dictionary rested. His eyes looked straight ahead so that nothing in his periphery could distract him and take him off-course. Of all the places on the school grounds—the mezzanine, the west entrance, the washrooms, and the parking lot—the library was one of the least popular. It was a forgotten ground where old stories and old library staff waited to die, but he often found himself there because books (and the characters within) were some of his closest friends. Here, words existed only on pages, and he was grateful for that silence. He also appreciated the Dewey Decimal System, comforted that every topic had its place and number and every book belonged some-where. When he reached the dictionary, it was already open and words commencing with *THR-* stared back him. He flipped through chunks of pages at a time, slowing down as he reached G. He momentarily paused at *game* and *garage* and *gavel* before finally arriving at *gay*. He scanned the small type quickly and shut the book.

He was surprised that the definition of *gay* included the words *merry* and *cheerful* because the word was always uttered like a grunt or a burp or a fart even, the kind of sound your body makes when it's trying to clear something out. As he walked away from the dictionary and toward the exit, he wondered if he seemed particularly merry or cheerful, and if so, why were these unlikeable traits?

He instantly thought about his family's most recent drive to Lahore Sweets & Restaurant.

*Stop laughing!* his dad had yelled, turning his gaze away from the road ahead and directly onto his eldest son in the back seat. Hoping to divert some of his dad's anger, he looked at his younger brother Shanth, who had told the joke about their Sunday school teacher at which they were both giggling.

*Why? With all the suffering in the world, it's good that we have a son who laughs so much,* his mom pushed back.

*Ever since his voice changed, his laugh... I can't listen to it.*

*Don't listen to your dad! Don't stop laughing, son,* his mom had said, turning around to look at him with the stern but caring expression that was generally reserved for the morning before a class presentation, the subtext: *You can do anything!*

As he left the library, he passed Ms Sinclair, the librarian. He had always admired her upright posture, despite her heavy mane of grey hair, and secretly thought of her as a witch—the good kind—because of her ability to know exactly which book he needed to complete, whatever assignment he was working on, or to satisfy his latest curiosity.

*Did you find what you were looking for?* she asked, predictably.

He didn't smile or respond politely as he typically would have.

The following week, he did his best to exemplify one different, non-cheerful mood each day, pretending he was auditioning for various roles in a play for an invisible panel of judges. On Monday, he was grumpy, which was easy enough because everyone is grumpy on Mondays. He did not style his hair or tuck in his shirt or say *thank you* when the bus driver handed him a transfer. On Tuesday, he was mournful. He wore all black and listened to Fiona Apple on his Discman. But the *you're gay*s persisted, regardless of the careful extraction of all things cheerful from his disposition. When Friday arrived, and he appeared exhausted, it was not an act.

*What's wrong?* Kevin asked.

Kevin Wheeler was one of the few males he knew who didn't seem to be preoccupied with his gayness. At least, not when they were on the morning bus together chatting about Kevin's latest stalker (whom he eventually would date), confiding about their ongoing family dramas, or flipping through the copy of *Playboy* magazine that Kevin had stolen from his older brother. He didn't care what he and Kevin talked about. For these thirty minutes, he cherished sitting close to another boy, imagining that this proximity and intimacy meant that he and Kevin were friends, he and Kevin were brothers. Once, he made the mistake of waving when he passed Kevin in the hall on the way to social studies. Kevin had looked right at him with an expression he had seen on the faces of other boys, eyes squinted and lips frowned, and then looked the other way. He never gestured at Kevin at school again. He understood that, at school, he was a liability that Kevin couldn't afford and felt grateful for their special bus time when Kevin could be his true self.

*I can't figure out why everyone keeps calling me gay.*

The *g*-word had never come up in their conversations before, and he had been thankful for this asylum. But after the week's defeat, he didn't have the motivation to make up a story about what was bothering him.

*It's the way you use your eyes*, Kevin responded, shrugging his shoulders as though the answer was obvious.

He spent that night staring at his eyes in the mirror, wishing he had asked Kevin to be more specific. The dictionary had made no mention of eyes, but could it be possible that something about the way he saw or blinked said *gay*? He began fantasizing about a life where he could see with his eyes closed and the *gay* was sealed under his eyelids, or rather, a life in which he couldn't be seen at all, free from the scrutiny of others. The next day, he tried to minimize eye contact, looking down for safe measure. But when he bumped into Chuck Treeman by the lockers, Chuck's response was, *You're gay!*

He attempted a different approach, this time paying close attention to the variables necessary to elicit a *you're gay* in the hope of uncovering a pattern. He was much more successful in this endeavour. *You're gay*s usually followed a display of weakness—like when he tripped or couldn't carry the stack of chairs from the back of the classroom to the front—or any behaviour or interest akin to that of his girl classmates. *You're gay* was a whip attempting to classically condition the weakness and the girl out of him.

Unfortunately, he was unable to accurately deduce what behaviours or interests belonged exclusively to girls, and therefore the whipping continued, determined to debilitate. The *you're gay* at the school assembly after he performed a pitch-perfect rendition of Vanessa Williams' "Save the Best for Last" muted the notes in his throat and the urge to create melody. The *you're gay* when he worked on his math homework in the loner corner of the cafeteria ensured that his concentration was shaken and consequently, that the most he would ever achieve in class would be Average.

The greatest blow was when *you're gay* found itself on the tongues of his friends, concealed in the form of a question.

*Ugh, those guys won't leave me alone! I hate boys!* he ranted into his parents' wooden duck-shaped phone.

*So, are you gay?* his friend Rosie Cipher responded coolly.

*What? Why? What does that have to do with anything?!*

*Well, you just said you hate boys. Maybe it's because you are attracted to them?*

*Attracted to boys?*

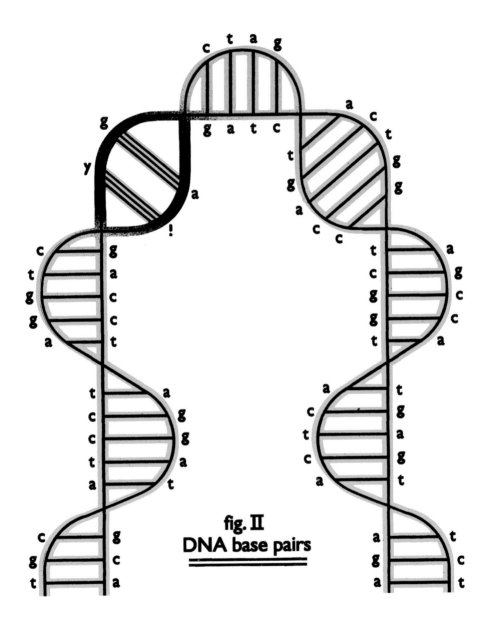

fig. II
DNA base pairs

His frustration subsided and turned to sickness. How could she have known that he did, in fact, think of Josh Madison, the class clown with the football-player build whose locker was conveniently across from his, when he jerked off? Did she know that he also thought about Rochelle Hunter, the wannabe prom queen with the breasts everyone wanted—perfectly round and noticeable, but not Hollywood excessive—or that, whenever the new girl from Lethbridge, the one with the labret piercing and the leopard-print jacket that she never took off, said his name, a bolt of heat shot up his lower spine?

He was beginning to understand that the parameters of *you're gay* existed beyond his body and extended to the very core of his desire. And if *you're gay* somehow named and shamed his specific desires, this had to mean that they were different. No one else was attracted to both boys and girls. His desires must be wrong.

Soon after, he caught a passing mention of the gay gene on the radio show that his dad listened to every morning. He put down his spoon and watched the O-shaped cereal swell up with milk, mirroring the swelling of his stomach. If indeed there was genetic printing, if the gay instruction existed at the molecular level, he feared that his condition festered deeper than he had imagined. Why had his parents not warned him about this defect they had passed on to him? Were there others in his family like him? Perhaps his cousin in India, the famous Bharata Natyam dancer, had the gay gene too? He knew these were questions he could never ask. His parents would never want to discuss the gay gene, especially in relation their son. And regardless, it was too late. He remembered the double-helix structure of DNA he had been shown in biology class and thought how appropriate that it looked like a chain.

What else could he do but return his surveillance to his body, which now appeared to him as ugly—and appropriately so. He told himself that every zit on his cheeks, forehead, nose, shoulders, and back was a punishment he deserved for the abnormality beneath his skin. He blamed his hands and their desire for touch, and in response, his hands lost their desire to touch his body at night. He tried to forget about his wrong penis, disgusted by both its misdirected longing when erect and its pathetic floppiness when soft, and in response, his penis shrivelled up, forgetting about him.

He wished that the *you're gay*s would forget him too. And in a way, they had. He began to hear the words even without words— in the chuckling in the mall food court, the murmurs behind him in the theatre, the staring on Whyte Avenue, and even in the silence of his bedroom, in his very own breath. He wondered about their hatred, which had become his hatred. Where did hatred reside? What did it look like? Was there a "hate gene" too? Was it the antithesis to the gay gene, its nemesis? Was it the cure? How could both genes coexist in one body, in his body? It seemed to him that one trait would have to recede at some point and the other express its dominance.

He stopped going to class regularly and was silent when he did attend, his hands rolled into fists in his lap even if he knew the answers. He stopped signing up for extracurricular activities, stopped spending so much time with his mother, and stopped seeking pleasure altogether. His world was reduced to bare necessity. Home was where he slept and ate, and school was where he learned.

He graduated from high school amorphous, his teenage body and its vast possibilities left on the unpaved field where it was first attacked.

◆ ◆ ◆

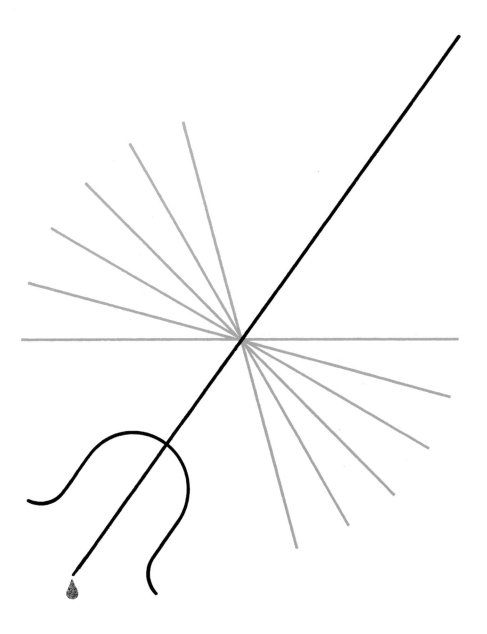

*Ganesh! Ganaphathi! Gadhadhara!*

Seeing my lifeless child on the doorstep where he had been on guard, what else can I do but cry his name over and over again? His name and new names, future pet names I didn't have the luxury of giving him, in the hope that one of them will reach him, wherever he is, and bring him back to me.

*Vingavinashaya! Vinayaka! Vishwamukha! Vingeshwara!*

I stop at the sound of my own name.

*Parvati, my love… You knew this boy?*

I turn around, and there is Shiv, back from hunting, his blue hue almost purple now.

*He was my own, my beloved, my son*, I wail.

*Your son? Our son? But how?*

I laugh at the redundancy of the question. He remembers. He remembers who I am and looks away. I follow his eyes to where his trishul, his weapon of choice, lies.

*You? You did this?*

I stand up and the sun sinks.

*He would not let me in. I didn't know. How could I have known?*

*YOU?*

He looks down. I close my eyes while the greatest betrayal buries itself beside my greatest loss. For a moment, it is as though all of the divine matter that makes up my form—stardust and intention—has dissolved, and I am pure, condensed feeling. Is this what it is like to be human?

Shiv is now on his knees, trying to bring the body and head together, as though such an obvious gesture is enough to revive Ganesh. How dare he? This demonstration of arrogance fuels me. Without contemplation, my feet begin to beat the ground, my body lifting and landing, cracking the walls and pillars that hold together our abode with the abundant force of my grief. I will bring every mountain down and raise every ocean, for without life, the life of my perfect child, there can only be destruction. Without Ganesh, there can be no Parvati, just Shiva.

I stop at the sound of my name. It is a name I have never been called before, but instinctively I recognize it as my own: *Uma.*

I turn around, and there he is, on his feet, standing, smiling. My Ganesh, alive, with the head of an elephant.

*Gajanana! Gajakarna! Gajavakra! Vakratunda!*

• • •

He didn't expect to feel this way.

He didn't expect to feel at all. But during the extended six-month break before university and his self-imposed exile from others, save for his family, his body's natural drive to regenerate solidified him into a new shape.

He and his body were now frenemies: His body provided him with services, getting him from point A to point B, and he, on good days, provided his body with motivation, a reason to get from point A to point B. They tolerated each other. Together, they had learned to tolerate the remaining *you're gay*s—the ones that still appeared occasionally at the grocery store and in his dreams—until they became synonymous with *I'm gay*.

It was strange, at first, to label his new self with a word that had been used as a weapon against him. But his new body still felt old curiosities that he found increasingly difficult to suppress.

The first time he said the words aloud, *I think I'm gay*, he ducked, expecting retribution from his brother or the ceiling or the walls around them.

*Oh. That's cool*, Shanth said.

*It is?* He looked up.

*I mean, you're my brother. I love you. It doesn't change anything.*

*It doesn't?*

*It just means now you can tell me if my butt looks good in jeans.*

After telling his brother, each time he said *I'm gay* it felt a little easier. He found that all of the characteristics that had set him apart from the other boys were conveniently explained and compartmentalized under

I'M GAY

Tori Amos fan/Watches *Beverly Hills, 90210*/Wears eyeliner/ Shops at The Gap/Likes to cook/Adores Mom/Has mostly female friends/Sings all the time

No justification necessary. Just a simple *I'm gay.* There wasn't much more that anyone wanted to say or do to him once he used their language.

When he told Sophie Reinhart, *I'm gay*, she squealed as though she had unwrapped her dream present on her birthday, and said he *had* to meet her friend, The Only Other Gay in Edmonton.

*You will have so much in common!*

The Only Other Gay loved being gay. The Only Other Gay had his own apartment and his own gay boyfriend and a stack of gay jeans that hit the ceiling. This made him feel even more self-conscious about his single pair of Levi's. Orange Tabs. Social suicide.

The Only Other Gay knew everything about being gay. Conversation generally centred around words like *top, bottom, cut, uncut* and questions like *Who does your hair?* and *What is your favourite Madonna CD?* He found out that he was a *bottom* because of his *slender build* and *feminine features* and would get used to having penises up his bum even if the thought terrified him. He wondered how gay he could really be when he couldn't relate to anything he was learning about his supposed self. For instance, what did circumcision have to do with being gay?

He also learned that *a gay with no community is a lonely gay.* This had to be true because he often felt incredibly lonely, even for friendship. Community meant going to The Only Local Gay Bar every Saturday night, where apparently, even more gays existed. It wasn't until he went to The Only Local Gay Bar with The Only Other Gay and watched as head after head turned and eye after eye stared at his new friend that he understood exactly why The Only Other Gay loved being gay. This place was the exact opposite of the world outside the bar—here it was possible to be liked.

Since he had been given the impression that The Only Local Gay Bar was exclusively for men, he was surprised to see women there.

*She is pretty… I kind of want to talk to her,* he said.

*About what? Where her shoes are from?* The Only Other Gay snapped.

*Do you think she likes boys?* he asked, ignoring The Only Other Gay's sarcasm.

The Only Other Gay laughed.

*Honey, we all liked girls at one point. But the Bi Highway always leads to Gaytown.*

Perhaps The Only Other Gay, who was clearly an expert on Gaytown, was right. He never mentioned women again. Instead, he focused on becoming the best gay he could be: his T-shirts got tighter and brighter, and he hoped that he too could one day command the same approval The Only Other Gay received.

Lately, though, something was happening inside his body, despite the *I'm gay*. He didn't immediately recognize it as attraction because transitioning from *you're gay* into *I'm gay* had also allowed him to stop having to think about, question, and sometimes be ashamed of his desires. *I'm gay* simplified them, reminding him that he desired boys and could wholeheartedly trust his renewed centralized hardening as The Measuring Stick.

But his body walked a bit faster every morning, the closer he got to work, hoping that the office would be empty so he could enjoy a private, deep inhale when he was welcomed by the lingering citrus scent of her perfume.

• • •

The sun rises and sets ten times before I finally let go of my son. I would keep holding him if his new ears didn't occasionally slap my face with their natural flapping.

Shiv and I aren't speaking, but not because I am still angry. How could I be? He was only looking out for me. But how can I justify the decapitation of a child? And how can he?

In the eyes of The Destroyer, does all destruction look and rank the same? As The Creator, I can certainly relate to this, for all creation is dear to me, belongs to me. But in the quiet of the night, when all my children are asleep, I secretly admit that Ganesh belongs to me a little bit more than the others do. While they are born from my will, Ganesh was made from my will and my body.

This is what still pains me, and this pain turns to speech.

*How could you not recognize me in him? How could you hurt me?*

*I am sorry*, he says, though he smiles a little out of relief. *I had been in a brutal battle, and when I finally reached home, this unknown boy refused to let me in. To our home!*

*So you cut off his head?*

*That's not how it happened.*

*Tell me then, Shiv. I want to understand.*

*I don't know how to say this. To admit this.*

*Admit what?*

He is silent, save for the hissing of the snakes around his neck. We are standing face to face, and I notice his attentive third eye is closed. Is it hiding from me?

*The truth is, I did recognize him,* he says softly. *Or rather, I saw you in him. How could I not?*

He pauses.

*You see, in those few moments, I was overcome with love for this beautiful child. For if he had somehow come from your body, I had to love him as I do your eyes, your laughter. Just as I love every extension of you. But, my dear Parvati…*

*But?*

*This was not just love.* He turns his back to me and sighs.

*If he had… somehow come from your body, he had to be closer to you, more precious to you. Once you had him, wouldn't you always be aware of our distance? What use could you have for me? What love would you have for an outsider?*

*Shiv…*

*I am sorry.*

*Shiv, I love you precisely because I didn't create you.*

• • •

He liked watching her from a distance.

He admired her indifference to her environment, as though everything and everyone existed only in relation to her and she alone determined their value. She would sing loudly in her office as though she was in her shower, completely unaware that her employees were listening, giggling. And yet, by being truly the centre of her own world, she seemed able to witness and appreciate the world around her—every structure and fallen leaf— with a genuineness that only someone who wasn't preoccupied with a constant internal dialogue of insecurity could possess. So when she complimented a friend, her motive wasn't secretly to elicit a compliment in return, and when she pointed out the tiny gargoyles seated on top of the Arts Building, it was with sheer curiosity and marvel, the kind he didn't have because he always looked down when he walked. And when he worked.

If only he had looked up, he might have noticed that she was watching him too.

They developed a morning ritual at the beginning of his shifts. She would sit down at the long table in the centre of the office and paint or file her nails as though this was just another task in her day's work. But they both understood that she was there, instead of in her office, to talk to him. He made efforts to file and photocopy—because he was somewhat invested in making a good impression as an employee, her employee—but his work was often derailed by an ever-growing, limitless list of questions he wanted to ask:

*What is your favourite colour? Where have you travelled outside of Edmonton? What are you thinking? Where do you like to shop? What is your sun sign? Where were your parents born? What book are you reading? What do you do on Saturday nights? What are you thinking? What are you thinking? What are you thinking? What are you…?*

He liked hearing her speak, the way she e-nun-ci-at-ed ev-er-y syl-la-ble, as though each one meant something. Their exchanges warmed up with the innocent *I did such and such on the weekend,* moved to the slightly more personal *I have this many siblings and pets,* and built to the existential *This is why I left my religion.*

Occasionally, the topic of her boyfriend Morty would surface, and he would listen attentively to every detail to learn as much as he could about the kind of creature that could captivate the captivating.

*So, what did you do this weekend?*

*Oh, Morty and I went to a toga party at his frat house.*

*What's a toga party?*

*A stupid party where everyone wears togas and gets drunk and high.*

*I can't imagine you in a toga. Though I suppose it's probably like a white sari?*

She laughed.

*I didn't wear one! But Morty did, of course.* She rolled her eyes.

He wasn't convinced of Morty's ordinariness by her description or even by Morty's any-white-male presentation when he came to visit her. Watching them walk away, hand in hand, he felt a sharp dislike, the kind he reserved for people he didn't know and therefore had the freedom to impose the worst qualities upon. But this dislike was coupled with a certainty that beneath his oversized, worn out, dried-ketchup-coloured waffle sweater, Morty possessed an exceptional quality, an old magic or skill found in the kind of book that was large, leather-bound, and printed in a Gothic font.

Eventually, their morning ritual extended to her walking with him to his psych class, after work. This didn't strike either of them as out of the ordinary because there was still so much more to say. Nor did the pace of the walk itself—the way their feet intuitively slowed down, stretching seconds into minutes, as they approached his class. Getting to know each other better and deeper in short increments led them to discover a shared love of movies.

*Have you heard about the new Baz Luhrmann film?*

*He has a new movie? Who's in it?*

*Nicole Kidman! And apparently she sings?*

*I love Nicole Kidman. And I loved* Romeo + Juliet. *It's one of my top five. And the soundtrack!*

*That Garbage song…*

They nodded in unison.

*Do you maybe want to see the new movie together when it's out?*

*I have always wanted a movie friend,* she said.

He imagined playing this role—sitting next to her for two hours in a dark theatre, sharing licorice and popcorn and laughter, and the riveting discussions that would inevitably follow about what he liked and what she didn't—and wanted nothing more.

•••

Destruction has a reputation for being chaotic and random, but the wisdom of Shiva tells a very different story. I know this better than anyone.

A long time ago, an uncomfortable alliance was established between demigods and demons. They were in search of the omnipotent nectar that was buried deep in the Ocean of Milk, a nectar that could restore some of the brilliance they had lost after years of battling each other. They understood, without fully grasping its breadth and mystery, that it was a risk to disturb the Ocean, but their thirst was greater than their caution. They churned the stubborn waters for days, and many surprises and secrets emerged, including the Wish-Fulfilling Tree and even Goddess Lakshmi. But no one had anticipated their search would trigger the release of the ancient poison that guarded the nectar, although, when I consider it now, it makes sense that the Ocean wouldn't surrender its greatest treasure without a fight. The mission halted as everyone panicked, understanding the danger they all faced if the poison wasn't contained. Then Shiv appeared and, without deliberation, drank the poison, holding it in his throat. Just like that.

Centuries later, during the Great Drought, the children of the Earth begged for Mother Ganga to descend from the heavens. Knowing that the planet was not strong enough to withstand the force of her passage from sky to land, Shiv agreed to be an intermediary between the two worlds, carrying Ganga's crushing, crashing weight in his hair.

*Why do you always say yes? Why do you always show up?* I once asked him.

*Death must happen in its own time, my love,* he responded. *Until then, I remain vigilant.*

This is why he spends so much time alone—because he is. No one, including myself, can comprehend the burden he carries, the balance that he holds, gracefully and without complaint. Has he ever thought of letting go? If he were to open his mouth and release the venom, take a break from the burning for just one day, everything would end. My body and all of my creations would ignite.

Today is the first day I have seen him cry.

• • •

Around the time his friends and family began to comment on how often he mentioned her—*Her this* and *She that*—she proposed that they meet outside of work, off campus. Hours before their meeting, he phoned his friend Geoff for a pep talk. Geoff listened as he swooned in phrases that sounded stolen from early '90s R&B slow jams:

*I can't get her out of my head.*

*I can't wait to see her.*

*She's so lovely.*

*But it's not a date or anything*, Geoff interrupted.

*No. She has a boyfriend.*

*No, I mean, you can't actually* like her, *like her, right?*

*I guess not? I don't know. I can't get her out of my head.*

He arrived at the coffee shop on Jasper Avenue exactly sixteen minutes before she did and took a seat facing the door so that they could see each other the moment she entered. But when she arrived, he looked down to give the impression that he was preoccupied with a very important thought. He slid his hands under his knees.

He looked up when her scent reached him. She smiled, and he jumped up to embrace her, a standard greeting amongst his friends, but when their jackets briefly touched, it felt more than friendly.

They sat down, and before she was able to unwrap herself from the layers of Edmonton winter-survival gear, the words stumbled out of him:

*I just want you to know that I dig you.*

There it was, sitting on the table between them, exposed for all of its unromanticness—the word *dig*. A teenage confession that prompted mutual teenage giggling for the next five minutes, but without eye contact. That kind of intimacy in this moment could heighten a *dig* to a *like*. And yet, his flushed cheeks revealed to him that he did, in fact, like her. *Like her*, like her. This was no friend crush.

Once the moment had passed and their faces stabilized, conversation flowed as effortlessly as it did when they were at work. But his confession had irreversibly changed how they looked at each other, or rather, enhanced it. The wool scarf around her neck, for instance, was suddenly indistinguishable from her skin and was completely irresistible to him.

• • •

*Uma! Uma! Uma!*

I rush over to where Ganesh is sleeping.

*Bad dreams again, dear one?*

I rock him back and forth in my arms. He barely nods, still half asleep.

*What happens in these dreams?*

*Someone is hurting me.*

After he falls back asleep, I hold him a little longer and then carefully ease myself up.

I turn around and see Shiv close behind us, pacing.

*Parvati, there is something I haven't told you. Something you haven't asked me.*

*I know.*

*You do?*

*I do.*

*Why haven't you asked?*

*Because it doesn't matter, he is still my precious boy. At least, it didn't matter…*

*I think you need to know.*

*I think you are right.*

*As you know, I had been in a battle… that day.*

We both wince. We have been trying to forget that day. Perhaps this is another reason why I had not yet asked the most obvious question.

*I was informed by the forest dwellers of an elephant king west of the mountains who had become greedy, claiming more and more of the land as his own. They said that his mind had turned black.*

*Shiv, no. NO.*

*I went to reason with him and to restore order. But—*

*NO. My son! But… how?*

*Do you recall that I wasn't able to reattach his original head? I didn't know what to do. I immediately thought of the last head…*

*That villain's head! You put that savage's head on my son's body?*

*I was desperate. I had to do something.*

*You had done enough! None of this would have happened if you had only…*

He tries to put his hand on my shoulder, but I step back.

*But that still doesn't make sense,* I continue. *Why was the union successful? How did he come back?*

*I don't know.*

*You don't know?*

*I honestly don't know. I think there was something about the energy in the room at the exact moment when head and body were put together.*

*Why don't I remember?*

*You were stomping, dancing hard, and everything was falling apart. Everything. But there was a distinct smell that cut through the air. Once I recognized it, I felt hopeful.*

*What smell?*

*It was you, my beloved. It was life.*

• • •

*The office needs a Christmas tree,* she announced.

The declaration came as a surprise to him because they had talked about how her family didn't celebrate Christmas and about her acute preference for all-inclusive holiday greetings at this time of the year. That he was one of the only staff members in the office when she made the announcement convinced him that this tree project was just an excuse for them to spend more time together, so he quickly volunteered to assist.

Maybe because this was something he had only ever done with his family, or because he was so particular about the tradition, but he felt there was something intimate about putting up a tree together—the careful winding of the screws at the base so the tree itself stood centred and the precise placement and distribution of the decorations to ensure that the lights were visible but the garbage-bag-green wires concealed. Thankfully, he had brought his copy of Christina Aguilera's *My Kind of Christmas.* Gleefully listening to her vocals, somersaulting higher and faster, reduced any tension between them.

They backed away from the small artificial tree, now lit and tinselled.

*We did it!*

*It's so beautiful.*

*It really is.*

His arm extended itself around her shoulder. She responded by putting her arms around his waist, and in this sideways embrace, they began to sway to the music. His body gradually turned in to face hers, their bodies clasping each other, growing into each other to form another tree. Limbs for branches, adrenaline for lights. They said nothing.

At the office holiday party, the memory of their special afternoon helped keep his jealousy at bay as he watched her boyfriend dote on her and, later that night, dance with her. After what felt like a respectful amount of time had passed, he asked her for the next dance. She accepted with a curt *okay*, as though she was doing him a favour, as though he was a worker asking his boss to dance at a holiday party. He responded by keeping as much distance between them as he could within the constraints of a slow dance. He didn't pull her close, and she didn't make eye contact. But he made her laugh by imitating his co-workers' clunky dance moves.

After their dance, they gave each other a forced smile, and he politely said *Thank you.*

She walked back to the table where her boyfriend was sitting. Morty looked at her curiously, as though he was seeing something he'd never noticed before.

*You know, if he wasn't gay, I would be really jealous right now.*

◆ ◆ ◆

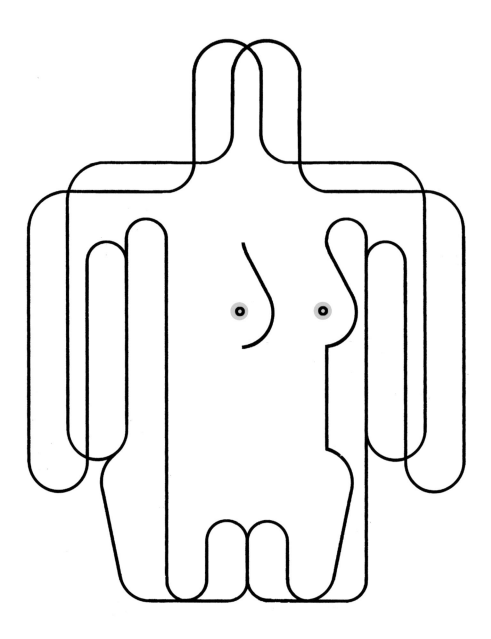

The first time she put her hand on his bare chest, he winced. And the second time.

They were under her desk, lit by the sparse glow of the computer screen above. Her playlist was on shuffle and by now had run its cycle at least three times. He wasn't paying close attention to the songs themselves, but each repeated song signalled the progression of a night he didn't want to end, even though his eyes were tightly closed and his legs trembling.

She had been slowly working at taking off his shirt, kissing the back of his neck as she rolled up the light blue fabric, and had finally succeeded. He felt as though all of his bones, his entire rib cage, were exposed.

After high school, his clothing had become a second layer of skin, a necessary fabric that protected his body from other bodies, a layer he removed only to change or shower or at the dreaded annual check-up with his doctor. But lying beside her, he drew courage from her body, her presence in every part of it. She did not possess the awkwardness he had witnessed in others, the uncertainty of their steps or the teenage stumbling that surfaced when they were faced with the inconvenient or unexpected. There was no apparent divide between who she was and her expressions, gestures, and movements; everything synced together in a gorgeous rhythm, like the perfect score to a perfect moment in a perfect film. Even her thoughts were clearly represented. In his spare time, he had been compiling a dictionary of all of her faces:

a.  single arched eyebrow: subject is unimpressed, skeptical. If in midst of joke, recognize its failure to be humorous and change subject. If in midst of disagreement, abandon hypothetical data and reframe with fact.

b.  fluttering eyelashes, eyes widened: subject is in a state of wonderment and will shortly follow with a flurry of questions, but they are mostly rhetorical.

c.  closed eyes: subject is not necessarily asleep, but rather potentially hyper-awake, as her true vision exists in her mind. Resist feeling neglected; subject is savouring.

d.

He had made comments about wanting to see the drawer where her underwear slept and wanting to photograph her nude. This was how he flirted with her—speaking outlandishly to test, push, and flatter, but always meaning it. Perhaps it was those comments that made her now gesture to her chest:

*Do you want to see them?*

*Of course I do.*

*They are big…*

*Of course they are.*

*No. Like really big.*

Warnings like this were given because he was gay. In a couple of weeks, he would, in turn, warn her that *This is not going to be a conventional relationship,* not really knowing what he meant, but trying to create some semblance of self-preservation in the event that he didn't measure up to the type of boyfriend with which she was better acquainted.

*I'll admit that Morty really knows what he is doing,* she had once mentioned.

*Oh?* he had replied, hoping that he sounded adequately interested, which he was. And wasn't.

*That's pretty much why I keep dating him.*

He tried to remind himself that her breakup with Morty was evidence that heroic sexual prowess was not paramount for her. But despite a lifetime of primarily female friends and a fondness for all-female-cast films like *Boys on the Side* and *Waiting to Exhale,* he was beginning to realize how little he knew about women, particularly about their anatomy. The Women's Network and its soft but mostly concealing body shots did not prepare him for this moment.

Her red scooped-neck shirt came off, followed by her black bra. They *were* big. He didn't realize just how much work a bra did and felt envious of its duty and intimate proximity to her body. He didn't want to stare and give her the impression that he was afraid or turned off, so he closed his eyes, cupped her breasts with his hands, and kissed them. He had read in the sex-advice column in *Men's Health* that men spent too much time focusing on nipples, so he tried to lavish an equality along the entire breast. He listened closely to the sounds she made as an aural compass to what made her feel good. He listened to the non-vocal cues too, where her body shivered. She also gently directed him, and he was grateful, especially when she guided his hand toward her pussy, an area he did not have the confidence to approach on his own.

He was intimidated by the secrecy of it, its depth. A penis felt comparatively obvious, an extrovert that just needed constant attention. But once his fingers were inside her, the immeasurable wetness produced waves inside his own body, and he found himself wanting to merge both sensations.

The first time she came, she laughed uncontrollably, her head tilted back into the pillow and the back of her hand against her forehead.

*Why are you laughing at me?*

*I am not…*

*Was it… okay? Did I do it right?*

*It was great!* She laughed again.

*Why are you laughing, then?*

*I just feel so fucking happy.*

They were on the floor again, this time at her vacationing friend's place, when they finally found themselves completely naked, side by side. Floors were easy to access, without parental supervision, and heightened the intimacy. Body and body and wood. Body and body and concrete. Body and body and carpet. Her touch was still painful to him, but now, instead of fearing it, fearing what her hands might discover—the ugly they might find, the coarseness of a terrain unclaimed or untravelled—he anticipated it. He desired it.

The first time he came, he apologized.

*Why are you sorry?*

*Was that okay?*

*Well, was it okay for you?* She squeezed his shoulder.

*Yes. Yes. It felt amazing.*

After years of hiding and being unseen, her touch was a deep thawing, a permission to feel, a memory of heat lost long ago.

◆ ◆ ◆

*When you were little, I was so worried you would end up fat like your dad, fat like an elephant.*

He had often heard about his fat childhood from his mother, about how his auntie had nicknamed him "Butterball" when his ten fingers became so plump that they joined into two lumpy mounds at the base of his arms. His mom had panicked and taken heed of a co-worker's advice that she switch his milk from homo to two-percent. Although his fingers separated again, her fear loomed over his teenage years, evidenced by her frequent descriptions of his childhood body as subtle warnings for his adult body. On the rare occasions he looked at himself in the misted bathroom mirror after showering, he cringed at the sight of his round belly, his mother's foreshadowing ringing in his ears. He was convinced that the words *fat* and *failure* were synonymous to his mother because, in her arguments with his dad, she would first attack his weight and then list the rest of his inadequacies:

# FAT
big-mouthed
overspender
selfish
careless
brainless

He tried to be stringent about what he ate, but when he visited his mother's family, his aunties all said the same thing:

*You are so skinnnnny! Doesn't your mother feed you?*

There was one body that caused him greater discomfort than his own—his dad's. His dad would often commence undressing as soon as he walked through the front door, celebrating the end of the work day by shedding layers of clothing throughout their home. *Dad!* he would whine, frantically picking up the discarded clothes, trying not to look as his dad marched around the house wearing only his torn-up, stretched-out briefs. *Why can't you change in your bedroom like everyone else?*

Even though, by definition, his dad's name, Sundar, meant beautiful, Sundar himself was repeatedly told otherwise by own mother:

*Sundar is fat like an elephant!*

Sundar had grown up in a home in which his mother was solely responsible for the food. Even though their servants were allowed to help by acquiring and grating and cutting and chopping and rinsing, the actual act of cooking belonged to her. This was more than just a sense of duty or birthright. In the kitchen, she could transform her love into something edible and sustaining for her six children. In the kitchen, her love was tangible and alive. Perhaps this was why Sundar felt closest to his mother here, watching her knead dough until it was smooth, roll it out into a perfect circle, and flip it on the skillet until lightly browned. Sometimes, before dinner was served to the family, she would secretly feed Sundar the rotis, wrapped around aloo mattar, with her bare hands. He felt guilty that his siblings had not yet eaten but, sensing his worry, she would smile and whisper, *It's best when it's fresh.*

Her smile receded as Sundar got older and his body expanded, mirroring her own enormity. Looking at him, she saw an animal, an elephant made of her own flesh, reflecting her own weight. She began to resent his constant need for nourishment and chastised him when he looked for food in-between meals. This only increased his hunger.

Sundar could taste the absence of his mother's love in the food. The roti was bitter, the pilau dry, and, no matter how hot the food was when served, the warmth and taste of the sun was gone. But he kept eating, hoping to find to her love once more.

• • •

We don't know how to be a family. Although I have forgiven Shiv, and Ganesh does not remember his beheading, the memory of violence lingers, a bloodstain refusing to be washed away. Shiv tries to earn our trust again by being more present, wandering off less, even in his own mind, and paying attention to our every word and need. Ganesh is still having nightmares, and Shiv is always the first to respond, singing songs about me to soothe Ganesh back to sleep.

*Jai Jai Devi Girija Matha*
*Jai Jagadambey Pranava Swarupini*
*Ashta Bhujangini Akhilaa Dhari*
*Jai Yogeeswara Hrudaya Vihari*

He does not understand that there are still days when I cannot bear to look at him, that it might be best for everyone if he returned to his former, mostly removed self.

At times, it is hard to look at Ganesh too. The knowledge of where his head comes from is not only a reminder of Shiv's actions, but it also makes it difficult for me to see Ganesh as one complete being. I recognize his body, the one born from my own, but not his foreign, animal head.

The other gods and celestial beings are not receptive either. Although anyone related to Shiv could be perceived as strange, however revered, Ganesh seems to push the limits of acceptance. I have even heard rumours that the moon mocked Ganesh, particularly his size. (I will obliterate the moon right out of the solar system if these rumours are true.)

Ganesh loves to eat. He befriended a mouse after an incident when both of them fought over the last modaka, only to bond over their common sweet tooth. Together, they consume all the daily offerings that are left at our doorstep by demigods and humans who seek our blessings. A friendship with a rodent only amplifies Ganesh's supposed strangeness, but if the others would only look more closely, they would behold a tender heart, able to love regardless of size or status or expectation. If I could reconstruct my own heart, I would make it identical to his.

I can't help but be mesmerized as I watch Ganesh eat. With every bite, the unrestrained joy in his eyes seems to grow once it reaches his belly, pushing it outward. I can almost taste the ladoo, jalebi, and rasgulla in my own mouth, the sweetness spreading throughout my core. Watching him eat unifies his head and body for me and allows me to see him as one.

Lately, I find myself wondering if this is partly what he has been trying to do for himself as well—using food to build a body in balance with his head.

• • •

In elementary school, he and his classmates drew the sun identically—an uneven circle in a top corner of the page with jagged triangles around the entire circumference, filled in with yellow crayon, and a smiley face drawn on it with an orange crayon. As she slept, he thought that, if he were to draw the sun now, it would be her face, not yellow but the colour of palaces in Jaipur. Her upturned lips that smiled even while she dreamed, not orange but the shade of eggplants, her crown of curly hair replacing the triangles, her eyes that were stars in their own right.

*But why draw her face when I can look directly upon it?* he wondered. Instead, something about her face made him want to sing. This response was more concrete than melody; it was a lyric too. A melody that had not yet been sung and a lyric not yet written.

Quietly humming, he followed the lines of her neck down to her shoulders, clasped by his hand, his arm around her back, their bodies held together by her white sheets. If he squinted slightly, together they appeared to him like a sea of brown rolling over and under white clouds.

He remembered trying to figure out what kind of brown she was when they first met. The shape of her nose gave away her Muslimness, but he wondered what type of brown girl wore khakis and had a crush on Data from *Star Trek*. He took clues from her closest friends when they visited her at work. They were *Brown Girl* brown; their approach to style, acquired mostly from Dynamite, Garage, or Forever 21, involved showing various degrees of skin and yet always appearing business-casual, as though they weren't able to completely shed their parents' traditionalism. They were professionals who dated only Muslim brown men and went to clubs that played hip hop music infused with some Bollywood. She really liked that one Nelly Furtado song.

He was in a brown category that was generally frowned upon by other brown people, especially other brown parents: *Alternative brown*. This meant he wore vintage clothing, had his ears pierced, had blond streaks, and hung out with non-browns.

In some ways, he was more brown than anyone he knew. When given the choice of restaurants to go to on his birthday, his craving for deep-fried cheese cubes mixed with peas trumped burgers or pizza. He listened to santoor on Saturdays when he cleaned his room and understood the complicated, often multi-storied significance behind most Hindu celebrations like Deepavali and Onam. He thought Sanskrit was the most beautiful language he had ever heard and found the constriction of English translations, which exposed the general apathy of English itself, deeply disappointing. "Prema" was so much more expansive and sacred than "love."

And yet, brown in and of itself, had not yet registered as a real colour to him. Brown was unremarkable, a non-colour, akin to a shade of grey. For he had been blinded by another colour: white. White expanded limitlessly and drained every other colour out until all that could be seen was

whitefriendwhiteactorwhiteteacherwhiteneighbourwhiteinve

ntorwhitestrangerwhiteactresswhitecoworkerwhitesingerwhite
principalwhitefriendwhiteactorwhiteteacherwhitecashierwhit
eneighbourwhitestrangerwhiteserverwhitepostmanwhiteclass
matewhitebullywhiterockstarwhitefriendwhitefriendwhiteking
whitequeenwhiteteacherwhitemodelwhiteconquererwhitesav
iourwhitewomanwhiteprimeministerwhitedoctorwhitereales
tateagentwhiteneighbourwhitefriendwhiteprofessorwhitegod
whiteairstewardwhitemanwhitescientistwhitedentistwhitewhite
whitewhitewhitewhitewhitewhitewhitewhitewhitewhitewhite
whitewhitewhitewhitewhitewhitewhitewhitewhitewhitewhite
whitewhitewhitewhitewwhitewhitewhitewhitewhitewhitewhite
whitewhitewhitewhitewhitewhitewhitewhitewhitewhitewhite
whitewhitewhitewhitewhitewhitewhitewhitewhitewhitewhite
whitewhitewhitewhitewhitewhitewhitewhitewhitewhitewhite

White was almost every interaction he had, and through this relentless exposure, he learned to value it, serve it, aspire to it, his white bedroom walls plastered with white famous faces. This was where the true power of white resided.

But something unexpected happened when he placed his brown next to hers, something that white worked so hard against.

whitewhitewhitewhite     brownbrown     whitewhitewhitewhite

In the absence of white, he could see colour.

*Your brown has more of a pink base than mine,* he had observed the first time they held hands, still looking for answers to her origin in her skin.

*It's true. And your brown has a yellowy tone to it,* she said.

*I look jaundiced?*

She laughed and shoved him gently. *No, no. You are golden.*

*I am also darker than you…*

*Your skin is perfect. Why would anyone want to be another colour?* She kissed his cheek.

Marvelling at her perfectly round chestnut cheeks, he couldn't help but agree. Falling in love with her brown had unexpectedly given his own skin new value, a new sheen.

As they dug past the surface, they discovered their brownness was a map that only directed them closer, pointing to their abundance of commonalities and fascinating variations. She called lentils "dhar," he called lentils "dhal." His motherland was India; she was a child of the Ismaili diaspora. She couldn't do a brown accent; he sang her songs in Kannada. Through these travels, they created a whole new shade of brown—their shade—one that beamed gloriously in the beauty of itself, one that hadn't been taught that it was anything less than extraordinary.

As she woke up to his face, she spoke softly in Khatchi:

*Aau thoke bo arathi.*

• • •

*What do you like about me?*

The question was unexpected. On its own, it implied an insecurity, forcing the other person to respond with a list of compliments:

*You are intelligent,*
> *sexy,*
> *hilarious,*
> *adventurous,*
> *thoughtful...*

Fishing was not her style, but before he responded he found himself envious that he hadn't thought to ask the question himself.

*Everything.*

He put his hand over her hand.

*That's not an answer.*

She pulled her hand away.

*But that's my answer.*

He didn't know how to say in words that she was the first person he had ever liked outside of his needs. He didn't like her because she was another person whose approval he craved or merely because she liked him back. He liked her for herself and every-thing she embodied.

But even more than this—before her, he hadn't known how to trust love because he had always had to work for it. Every smile, phone call, birthday gift, he had fought for. Put out his neck for. Stood in the rain for. Earned with muscle and memory. He noticed the details no one else paid attention to, remembered the occasions that everyone else forgot, weathered rejection or no response at all, found a void, and then found a way to fill it.

So when someone had said *I need you*, it just meant he had been successful. If they didn't need him, he hadn't bent low enough, gotten on his knees, and his skin hadn't developed the right callouses.

When they said *I miss you*, it just meant that they were respond-ing to the gaps between his carefully timed, repetitive appear-ances in their inbox or on their doorstep.

And when they said *I love you*, he wanted to respond: *You should*. And then walk away.

But not with her. With every step he had taken toward her, she had taken a step toward him.

His hand reached for her hand again.

*No, really, what do you like about me?* she insisted.

*Why?*

*I figure if I know, I can keep doing it to keep you for as long as I can.*

• • •

The birth of my second son, Muruga, has healed our familial wound. He is a new beginning for us, a new and unsullied body at whom to direct our love, reflecting back the best in all of us. So content are we to be in each other's company that we seldom leave our abode.

*Shall we play a game, boys?* Shiv asks.

Muruga jumps up. *Yes!*

*Okay. Whoever is the fastest to circle the earth three times will receive a special blessing from your mother and me,* Shiv says.

*Shiv, you know we love our boys equally.*

Muruga hops on his peacock vehicle and bolts off without hearing my admonishment.

I know Shiv has to be jesting about the reward, but Muruga has the advantage. Comparisons have been made between Muruga and Ganesh in the celestial and human worlds, and it is clear that Muruga is everyone's favourite. Is this because of Ganesh's now even larger physicality? Although he is perfection to me, I recognize that, of the main deities, he lacks an immediate prettiness. His skin isn't the colour of the sky. He can't be beautified (or hidden) by flower garlands. His presence is unabashedly what it is. Isn't that what divinity should be? The embodiment of truth?

I turn to Ganesh, who is slowly rising to his feet.

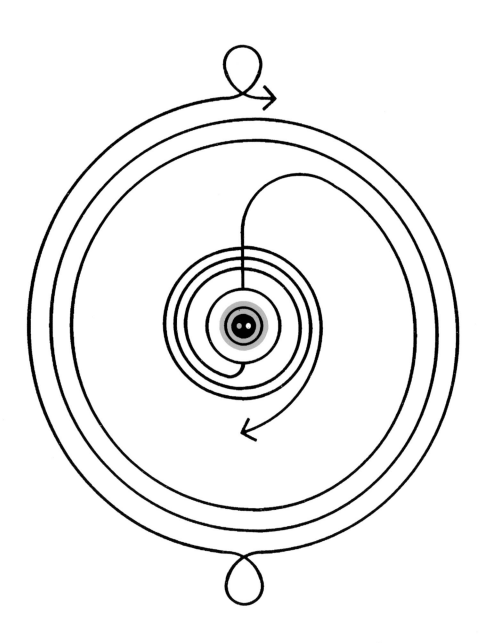

*Your father is being silly. You don't have to play.*

He doesn't respond. Instead, he walks solemnly toward where Shiv and I are seated, leaning on each other, and begins to circle us in silence.

*Ganesh, what are you doing, son?*

After three rounds, he finally responds, panting.

*Dearest Uma and Pita … you are my earth. You are my world.*

I put my hand on my chest and sigh. Shiv stands to embrace Ganesh.

*Oh, beloved son. You have demonstrated how a loving heart and a wise mind can surpass any physical prowess. From this day forward, no prayer or journey may commence without acquiring your blessing first. I name you Lord of the Lords.*

• • •

*Do you want to look at the stars tonight?* she asked.

He responded with an enthusiastic *yes* into the receiver.

This had become one of their cherished pastimes. She would drive them somewhere secluded, usually by the man-made pond behind the Millwoods sign, and park the car. They would recline their seats, and instead of looking through the sunroof that her car did not have, they would stare at the grey fuzzy roof and let the currents circulate.

His mixtape through her tape deck.
The lyrics onto her lips,
the melody lingering in her throat.
Her voice in his ears, quickening his pulse, shooting down
into his left palm covering her left thumb.
Their breathing united in a growing fog.

On the nights that they wanted more from the music, to twist their bodies into each other against a hard and constant beat, they went dancing. It was awkward at first, going to The Only Local Gay Bar together as a couple. But he preferred being in a space where his moves weren't limited to the general male domain of shoulder shrugging and head bopping, where he could transfer the reins of his body to the music without worrying about getting called *sissy*, and she felt relieved to be in a space where she wasn't having to give the phone number of the local pizza delivery to men who asked her breasts out, so it kind of worked out.

In addition to stargazing and dancing, in the past four months there had been road trips to Calgary, the exchange of birthday presents, secrets, sweat, and spit, and the finishing of each other's sentences. She complained about the latter, worrying about what it meant to have someone else so attuned to the very private sanctum of her internal dialogue.

He worried too.

After every day they spent together, it became easier to envision another day and harder to endure the days apart. On days when he was less careful, he allowed himself to daydream. Who could they be outside their parents' homes? Who could they be outside of university? Maybe they would move to Vancouver; she loved the ocean, and he loved every city that wasn't Edmonton.

But the graver question for him was one that loomed throughout his daydreams, diffusing them: *But aren't I gay?*

If he were gay, something had to be missing between them, even though, when he examined his heart, looking for gaps, inconsistencies, or moments of unhappiness, it appeared fuller now than it had ever been. So he examined her.

*What about him?* He pointed at the man wearing the faded baseball hat, crossing the street ahead of them.

*No way. He looks like Joey from* Friends.

*What about him? He looks like your type.*

*What is my type?*

He imagined her much happier with an older, smarter, bulkier man, a professor. She would live with him in a spacious, sunlit loft in Montreal, with a wall of philosophy and science books. His name would be Bernard or a hyphenated French name like Jean-Luc or Marc-André. Bernard would wear rugby sweaters and thick framed glasses and could confidently converse about cars and hockey with her brother and dad.

*Don't you wish I was more manly?* he asked.

*You are a man,* she responded.

*No, but like…a real man. A man that doesn't know all the words to* The Little Mermaid *soundtrack. A man that isn't attracted to other men.*

*I love when we sing together. And being attracted to other men doesn't make you less of a man. It's actually pretty hot.*

*You know what I mean…*

*No, I don't.*

When she didn't give him the answer he expected, when *I'm gay* didn't mean he was somehow lacking or inferior in her esteem, he was forced to revert his inspection back to himself.

In his stomach, he couldn't shake the feeling that he was maybe a fraud, lying to her and lying to himself, despite his honesty. After all, how could he know if his feelings were in fact genuine and not just some part of him still resisting *I'm gay*?

He had also never kissed a boy, let alone dated one, and while he couldn't imagine what could feel better than her lips and his lips, he didn't feel informed enough to dismiss the potential of his lips and another his lips. *I'm gay* meant that a part of him felt that there must be a better, truer kiss waiting for him, somewhere.

So how could he keep kissing her?

• • •

The next three minutes would determine the course of the rest of his day. One hundred and eighty seconds turned into dots that needed to be connected and interpreted, a task he would commit himself to during sociology, on the forty-minute bus ride home, and probably while he watched *Party of Five*. He would call her, and together they would discuss what the final result of his day's analysis meant and how best to prepare for next week.

Post-breakup, they were slowly transitioning into friendship. They still weren't able to prevent their hands and mouths from fastening onto each other, but they independently and unusually decided not to talk about it. Instead, they interpreted talking about other romantic interests as an adequate indication that they were moving on.

He stopped on the side of the corridor that bridged the law building to the university mall and pretended to look for something inside his bag, but what he was looking for was up ahead. Any second now, That Guy was going to walk by.

They would do the gay dance with their eyes—stare, look away, stare, look away—each modelling for the other's hidden camera. No smile, in case the other wasn't gay or wasn't interested. In Alberta, the combination of a stare and a smile, from one man to another, however brief, could be dangerous. He couldn't allow himself to forget this.

That Guy's unpredictability only heightened his attraction. Last week, That Guy had barely made eye contact, mostly looking at his phone. The week before, That Guy had slowed down and licked his lips as though he was getting ready to say something. What was That Guy going to say? How would he respond? He would probably first pat the back of his head to make sure his cowlick was not too visible and shake his bangs to make sure his new pimple was properly concealed.

What he wanted was more than a stare, more than an exchange of words, more than to see or touch what was beneath the cotton and denim.

He wanted to feel the validation of a man's desire. And not just any man's. He wanted to be desired by The Man He Deemed Desirable. When distracted in Shakespeare 101, he scribbled in his notebook:

*If I made you King*
*and you named me your Prince—*
*Then who is King*
*and who is Prince?*

If That Guy, whom he had chosen, liked him, thought he was good and worthy and beautiful, perhaps he too could think he possessed these qualities. Perhaps he could even like himself.

Or better, he could forget about himself completely. If only the connected dots materialized into a mask and cape that allowed him to transform into That Guy. To be able to fill out his clothing like That Guy, instead of having fabric gliding down his bony build like oversized drapes. To be able to walk with a sway-free, heterosexual coordination, in full military control of his shoulders, arms, hips, quads, and heels. To have a slim but elegant nose, one that conveyed confidence, instead of the gluttonous mound with two giant open windows for nostrils he had inherited via his dad from the motherland. To be learning the secret language of Law, which would lead to a model future championing justice by day and resting in a three-storey home at night, instead of pouring over the work of dead English poets, searching for (or, more accurately, hiding from) the answer to the most important question in the world: *What do you plan on doing with your Arts degree?*

To be the guy that another guy waits for, every Wednesday, from 12:30 to 12:33 p.m.

• • •

*You are going to be my boyfriend.*

These were the first words Smith said to him, the first time they met at a mutual friend's birthday party.

This forwardness surprised him, but the prophecy itself did not. Smith was a celebrity dancer, often featured in the local news, and with each Smith sighting, each mention of Smith's name in conversation, it never felt like a random occurrence, but rather a step toward each other. It wasn't a feeling of destiny, of future promise, as he was certain that Smith was out of his league, but a feeling of familiarity, as though maybe in their childhoods they had attended the same school or had played in the same park.

In person, Smith was even more attractive—the magnetism of his physicality enhanced by his character. His brown hair was precisely parted and his matching brown eyes were surrounded by lines of kindness, as though his eyes genuinely cared about every subject upon which they fell. His hands gestured delicately when he spoke, adding an element of dance to everyday conversation, and though he was a commanding six foot three, he never seemed unapproachable, always the first person to say *hello*.

He wasn't sure if hanging out with Smith qualified as "dating" because, when Smith wasn't talking about how much he adored his border collie and his family, he talked about his ex-boyfriend. It had not been an amicable breakup, and Smith was brokenhearted. But Smith was the first boy he had ever hung out with/dated, so it was easy to ignore Smith's condition and start imagining their shared life. He would work at the downtown

library during the day while Smith rehearsed. On Wednesdays, they would meet for lunch at the Korean restaurant where Smith used to be a server. Their evenings would be spent reading, his head on Smith's shoulder, on the second-hand loveseat in their small but well-designed apartment. He would get over his fear of dogs and stock up on lint rollers. He would attend Smith's every performance, watching from stage-side with a bouquet of pink roses to give to his man.

The first time he saw Smith's penis, they were on Smith's couch, arms around each other, lips against each other's. *Oops!* Smith said, signalling down with his eyes. Poking out from the waistband of his pants was what looked like a large pink thimble. He wasn't sure what to do at this point, if anything, aside from observe. Even that he wasn't sure of, and he had to remind himself: *It's okay to look.*

Smith recognized his paralysis and pulled down his own pants and white briefs. It stood proudly between them. As he gazed at Smith's penis, he couldn't help but think of his own. This comparing and contrasting seemed to be an inevitable by-product of having sex with a man.

Many of the differences in their physical attributes could be explained by their racial differences. When Smith took off his black T-shirt, he nodded with a feeling of déjà vu. Every shirtless male body he had seen, save for the males in his own family, had looked like Smith's: lean but muscular, smooth chest, hard stomach. Smith's body was every man's body. In *GQ*, the Sears catalogue, movies, and porn, he had digested copies of it countless times. He expected it. He worried about Smith's expectations, given that Smith had most likely never seen a naked brown body before. Before her, just the idea of the words *naked* and *brown* together had seemed incongruous, even to himself.

Being brown meant he had much larger nipples, two puffy Hershey's Kisses, and an abundance of hair everywhere. When Smith later jerked off both of their penises, he was uncomfortable with how much darker his penis was than Smith's. He was convinced that if their penises were at war, his penis would be typecast as the evil one, the villain.

What bewildered him most about being intimate with another man was the absence of the *Eureka!* moment he had been anticipating and had even been promised by gay males he knew, now that he was finally with the right sex, the same sex.

*Don't worry. Once with you're with a man, everything will make sense*, they had said.

But there was no great confirmation of his homosexuality with Smith either through
more frequent orgasms,

                                    or harder erections

           or the sound of trumpets

                or a sweeping feeling of superior satisfaction

or freedom

                    or truth

                          or home

or peace.

When he put his lips around Smith's penis or pushed his own penis into Smith's firm ass, he felt an undeniable pleasure, but not undeniably more than the pleasure he had experienced with her.

It was just different.

• • •

In the minutes before sunrise, when Smith's desk, bookshelf, and their pile of clothing on the floor would gradually bear the light of a new day, he found himself thinking about her. Missing her. Her face, the colour of palaces in Jaipur. Her upturned lips that smiled even while she dreamed, her crown of curly hair, her eyes that were stars in their own right.

• • •

**SATI**

Even in my human life, my heart belonged to Shiv.

Long before Ganesh and Muruga were born, I chose to be born to a human family. For years, they had had difficulty conceiving, and I was a gift, unbeknownst to them, for their generations of great piety. They named me Sati.

From an early age, I was captivated by the stories of the recluse god who lived in the mountains, even though my human father despised him:

*He wears only the skin of a leopard.*

*And the crescent moon in his hair.*

*He refuses to speak—to anyone! How arrogant!*

*Why is he a god? What is so great about him?*

Being mortal clouded my memory. I didn't know who I was or who Shiv was, but I knew I was drawn to his alien-ness, perhaps because he embodied the disconnection I too felt to my human body. Every night, I prayed:

*Dear Lord Shiva:*

*Please appear for me.*

*I adore you.*

Another reason that I had adopted a human life was that we both agreed it would be a new way for us to experience each other, love each other. From the day I was born, Shiv was equally captivated by my human form and its vulnerability, and watched over me from above like a second father. He was amused by my devotion to him and couldn't help but entertain himself further at my expense. Occasionally, he would appear in my peripheral vision and then suddenly disappear so that I would think that I was imagining him everywhere. This only heightened my yearning for him.

To celebrate and bless my coming of age as a woman, my father arranged a ceremony and feast, and everyone from the town was invited. The gods were invited. For every day that passed, I added one brightly coloured flower to my hair in anticipation of meeting Shiv. On the day of the event, my entire head was covered in a crown of flowers.

My father walked me into the hall toward the blazing sacred fire, which was surrounded by priests cloaked in cream-coloured robes, chanting loudly in unison. I scanned the hundreds of faces, friends and distant relatives, trying to find the one blue face that mattered.

Before I sat down, I whispered to my father:

*I don't see Shiva. Do you think he will come?*

*Shiva? Ha! Why would I invite that freak?*

*He wasn't invited? But all the gods were invited. It would be a grave insult…*

*Sati, now is not the time.*

*You are just jealous that his greatness surpasses yours, aren't you!?*

The fire rose and crackled with the sound of my voice.

*Silence, Sati.* My father motioned me to sit at the front of the hall next to the chief priest.

As the prayers continued, I gazed at the fire ahead, comforted by the only presence in the room that understood my burning sense of betrayal and disappointment.

How could my father be so cruel? And so foolish? Without Shiv's presence, the ceremony would be inauspicious. Cursed, even. Surely now I would never meet Shiv.

Contemplating my misfortune, I became mesmerized by the streaks of blue in the flames until all I could see was blue.

*Shiva! There you are! I knew you would come*, I said. I stood up and walked into the fire, arms open. This was the end of my human life.

Shiv, who had been watching the ceremony from above, swept

down to pull me out of the fire, hoping to bring me back to life. *Wake up, Sati, wake up!* he yelled, lifting my body into the sky. His own body vibrated like thunder, trying to re-energize mine.

Shiv circled the earth with my lifeless body folded over his shoulder for years. He forgot who he was, forgot the commonness of death, and in the process, forgot who I was. Although my human body had died, I of course had not.

I waited patiently for him in Kailash, not wanting to disturb him. I was fascinated by—perhaps even jealous of—his strange attachment to this human body. What was so special about it that it had deluded him? What was so special about it that he had forgotten that his beloved Parvati still lived?

Every morning, when the sun arose, my first words were to him, in my heart: *Wake up, Shiv, wake up…*

He never heard me. As I watched day after day surrender to darkness, I pushed against the urge to do the same.

As years turned into decades, the other gods and demigods began to lose their own sense of self and purpose watching the Lord of Destruction so confounded. For the sake of order, my brother Narayana intervened. He shot his golden discus into the air and sliced Sati's body into pieces. Seeing the hideousness of the human body cut up, Shiv remembered its expendability and immediately returned to his mind. And to me.

The first thing he said, without my even asking was, *I needed to know what it would be like to lose you.*

• • •

*What are we doing?* His eyes were determined and focused on her.

*We are talking?* She was just as focused, but on her plate, her closed mouth moving leisurely in a circle, savouring the slice of pumpkin cheesecake they were sharing.

*Don't you think this tastes like… clouds?* she continued, her tone as light and airy as her metaphor.

*No, seriously. What are we doing?* He stayed on course, dropping any lightness in his voice.

*Eating cheesecake?*

*No. I mean you and me. Us,* he said slowly, careful not to exude impatience.

*Oh.*

She put her fork down.

*I miss you. Like, really miss you.*

She looked up.

*What are you saying?*

They had always blamed biology, namely his biological gayness and the destiny that implied, for their inability to be together, to stay together.

*I am saying, what if we gave this a shot? A real shot.*

It was also biology—their elevated heart rates, their perspiration, and the dilating of their pupils when in each other's presence—that had made being just friends impossible.

*How would that be different from before? How would we not end up in the same place? You're gay…*

Their explicit physical responses to each other's pheromones, appearances, voices, and brains: her wet vagina, his erection.

*I don't know what I am. I know that I have dated boys and slept with boys, and I still want you. My body craves you.*

Based on the evidence, it wasn't logical to consider biology as the reason to continue living in the shadow of The Great Love That Couldn't Be.

If anything, it was a reason to get back together.

• • •

*This will be the last winter I spend in Edmonton.*

While he shovelled his parents' driveway, refusing to wear the toque his dad had given him because it would mess up his hair.

*This will be the last winter I spend in Edmonton.*

While he waited for a bus that he had most likely missed and anticipated waiting another thirty minutes for the next one.

*This will be the last winter I spend in Edmonton.*

While he sat on his hands in her parents' car, desperate for heat, knowing that neither his hands nor the car would ever be truly warm again for the next six months.

This was his attempt at what his mom called *manifestation*, a technique he resorted to out of desperation. Edmonton's cold grip felt inescapable as he watched his friends and peers already buying property or cars or starting their full-time jobs or their master's degrees at the University of Alberta. He didn't know what came next for him, but he knew whatever it was, it began with a departure.

He entered Toronto for the first time on the packed airport shuttle. It was a grand but intimidating welcome, the city guarded by billboards, skyscrapers, and glass condos. He couldn't figure out if the city was trying to keep its inhabitants in or keep visitors out or both. Looking through the window, he felt himself disappear into what he saw—the endless concrete and the traffic.

It was this feeling of forgetting himself, or rather the version of himself that had never fully adapted to Edmonton, and the possibility of creating a new and better version of himself, that cemented his decision to move to Toronto a month later.

Convincing her to move wasn't difficult. She shared his frustration with living in a city where there was only one street, one bar, and one theatre where you would inevitably run into the one person you didn't want to see. She couldn't move right away because of her work contract but promised to join him as soon as she could.

He signed the lease for a decently priced bachelor on Huntley Street with the hope that the large balcony, which was half the size of the unit, would have space for a small swing where she could read and rock, facing the sunset. He furnished the apartment minimally, not just because he knew this place would be temporary.

In his parents' home, the furniture and accessories were the real inhabitants, a vase or frame or chair compulsively planted in every corner, as though there was an underlying fear of empty space. He suspected it had to do with his mom's obsession with not appearing poor, every piece declaring their family's financial respectability. He felt a sympathetic suffocation for their house and told himself that he would always place importance on function first, that his future homes would be built around needs, his needs, versus appearance. He bought a futon that acted as a couch by day, a bookshelf that was also used as a workstation, and a coffee table where he ate all of his meals. The sole decorative presence was the sheer silver curtains, which let in just enough daylight and reminded him of her large collection of silver earrings.

Three months later, when she walked into the apartment, now their apartment, for the first time, he watched her face carefully, hoping she would approve of the choices he had made.

*I love it.*

*But?*

*I really love it. It's perfect. But…*

He laughed.

*We can't sleep on a futon. We are adults. We need a bed.*

A bed seemed to him a luxurious purchase. As he assisted her with the assembly of the headboard, he tried to ignore the futon behind them, now reassigned to play solely the role of couch. He was convinced the decision was less about adulthood, comfort, and her supposed back pains, and more about a personal grudge she had against the futon. Whenever they watched a movie, she would wriggle around on it for minutes, tackling different poses before settling with a loud sigh. But he was so happy to have her around all the time that he would have been delighted to throw the futon over the balcony if she so desired.

He loved seeing her toothbrush leaning on his, like miniature figurines of themselves with clear, bristled faces. It pleased him to know that, from nine to five, while their physical bodies were functioning in distant cubicles, acquiring money to pay their bills, their toothbrushes stayed still and close in that steel cup. It didn't matter that the cup itself was filthy at the bottom from the dried-up water because they were in it together.

The toothbrush feeling, however, was sometimes interrupted by the dishes feeling or the laundry feeling.

*I thought it was your turn?*

                              *I thought it was your night?*

Together they were learning not to underestimate the catastrophic power of a stack of soiled plates and cutlery or a basket of unsorted, clean socks and unfolded towels.

Under the strain of the necessary, everyday duties, they regressed, reverted.

She became a woman who was born in Tanzania and later banished from her home country. A woman who fell in love with a solemn and graceful man who sometimes preferred his solitude to her efforts to captivate with her daily account of a compilation of facts acquired from *People* magazine, *The View*, and word of mouth. A woman whose bustling bordered on comedy and who was therefore easily dismissed. A woman whose response to friction, or to her own sadness, was to walk away, shut the door, hole up.

He became a woman who was the second youngest daughter but the most responsible and therefore overloaded with tasks from her parents and siblings. A woman whose idea of loving was rooted in a quiet sense of duty, even when the request was unreasonable. A woman who often said *yes* either out of a sense of karmic obligation or a genuine inability to say *no*. A woman whose kindness and generosity were unmatchable and therefore caused a perpetual resentment which, at times, was volcanic, her love bursting out as lava.

He always knew when he was transforming into his mother because all of his surroundings would be covered by a pungent red hue. Then he would brew and stew until a faint smoke emerged from his nostrils.

*I don't want to come home to this mess. I don't,* he said. *It's disgusting.*

She would grow quiet, like her mother, her waters freezing over until completely solid. He wondered how she could ice him out.

*Aren't you going to say something? Or are you just going to sit there?*

She wondered how he could be so scalding. Each of their temperatures only intensified in response to the other. In the first months of living together, one of them would somehow find a means to moderate the other. She used reason:

*I do all the cooking, right? Doesn't it make sense for you to do all the dishes?*

He used shame:

*Since when do you cook? We eat out almost every night.*

But it never felt like a victory, the melting of ice, the extinguishing of fire.

It was by accident (and by chance), in a disagreement about something minor that neither of them would remember in a week, that he blurted the timeless and truest coming-of-age phrase: *I don't want to be my mother.*

They paused.

*Neither do I*, she responded.

This realization dispelled the argument, their attentions now elsewhere, brainstorming about how they could have conflict in their own way, instead of merely performing behaviours they had observed in their respective childhood homes.

*When you are mean, where is that coming from?*

> *I never want to be mean, especially not to you.*

*When you shut down, I get more agitated.*

*I need time to think before I engage.*

*What if you think aloud? Tell me what is going on inside you.*

*What if we took a ten-minute break instead?*

*Ten minutes is an eternity when I am hurt.*

*But you know I would never want to deliberately hurt you, right?*

They decided that the key lay in the window of time between each of their transformations. The person who had not yet turned would somehow have to find a way to cross the dividing lines unseen, get close enough in emotional proximity to shake the other with the crucial reminder: *We are on the same team!*

Other variations included:

*This is me, remember? Remember me?*

or

*I don't want to fight about _____, I love you.*

These worked every time.

• • •

It had started again.

## SCENE ONE
*(Setting: Nightclub, outside patio—stranger approaches one of his friends)*

Stranger 1: *Is he your friend?*
Friend 1: *Yes.*
Stranger 1: *Is he single?*
Friend 1: *No, that's his partner.* (points at her)
Stranger 1: *Ha! No way, she's just his fag hag.*

## SCENE TWO
*(Setting: Their workplace—two of her co-workers having lunch in the lunch room, third co-worker at microwave, overhearing)*

Co-worker 1: *He is trying to pass for straight now. I kind of feel sorry for him.*
Co-worker 2: *I actually feel sorry for her. I don't think she knows.*
Co-worker 1: *Is that why she looks so sad and fat?*

## SCENE THREE
*(Setting: A restaurant—two of their mutual friends face each other, sharing dessert)*

Mutual friend 1: *They must have an open relationship…*
Mutual friend 2: *Either that or they don't have sex.*

Perhaps because he had been hearing it most of his life, the subtext was unmistakably clear:

*You're gay, you're gay! YOU're gay, you're gay, you're gay, you're GAY, you're gay, you're gay, you're GAY, you're gay! you're gay, you're gay! you're GAY, You're Gay, you're gay, you're gay, YOU're gay, you're gay, you're Gay, you're gay, you're gay, YOU're gay, you're gay! you're gay, You're Gay, you're GAY, you're gay. You're gay, you're gay! YOU're gay, you're gay, you're gay, you're GAY, you're gay, you're gay, you're GAY, you're gay! you're gay, you're gay! you're GAY, You're Gay, you're gay, you're gay, YOU're gay, you're gay, you're Gay, you're gay, you're gay, YOU're gay, you're gay! you're gay, You're Gay, you're GAY, you're gay. You're gay, you're gay! YOU're gay, you're gay, you're gay, you're GAY, you're gay, you're gay, you're GAY, you're gay! you're gay, you're gay! you're GAY, You're Gay, you're gay, you're gay, YOU're gay, you're gay, you're Gay, you're gay, you're gay, YOU're gay, you're gay! you're gay, You're Gay, you're GAY, you're gay. You're gay, you're gay! YOU're gay, you're gay, you're gay, you're GAY, you're gay, you're gay, you're GAY, you're gay! you're gay, you're gay! you're GAY, You're Gay, you're gay, you're gay, YOU're gay, you're gay, you're Gay, you're gay, you're gay, YOU're gay, you're gay! you're gay, You're Gay, you're GAY, you're gay. You're gay, you're gay! YOU're gay, you're gay, you're gay, you're GAY, you're gay, you're gay, you're GAY, you're gay! you're gay, you're gay! you're GAY, You're Gay, you're gay, you're gay, YOU're gay, you're gay, you're Gay, you're gay, you're gay, YOU're gay, you're gay! you're gay, You're Gay, you're GAY, you're gay. You're gay, you're gay! YOU're gay, you're gay, you're gay, you're GAY, you're gay, you're gay, you're GAY, you're gay! you're gay, you're gay! you're GAY, You're Gay, you're gay, you're gay, YOU're gay, you're gay, you're Gay, you're gay, you're gay, YOU're gay, you're gay! you're gay, you're gay, you're gay! you're GAY, You're Gay, you're gay, you're gay, YOU're gay, you're gay, you're Gay!*

And yet, he resisted this translation out of genuine bewilderment at who was saying it: other gays.

He found it strange, alarming even, to be reminded of something he was implicitly aware of, namely his own desires. Did they think he had forgotten or that they were aware of something about him that he wasn't? At first, he was certain that the confusion arose from language; more specifically, the failure of language. He had refused to call himself *straight*. There were too many coffee breaks fantasizing about hairy chests to account for. But, conversely, calling himself *gay* rendered his love and relationship an illusion, an experiment, an exception.

So he abandoned language altogether (although, if pushed, he would state that that he was Hersexual, she being the immediate house of his desire and happiness). But with the absence of language, of a label, came an unfortunate implication: shame. To not commit to a label, however committed he was to his relationship, was to be

                indecisive

which meant

                    confused

which meant

                        closeted

which meant

                            GAY.

He anxiously waited for the right moment to come out to the other gays as being in love with a woman, which felt remarkably similar to when he would come out to the straights as gay: the

fear of condemnation, the waiting for the inevitable smirk or
narrowing of eyes or flurry of questions that were actually comments, which usually started with a
*But*
followed by
> have you considered that

and/or
> maybe you are scared

and ending with a question mark, that if put into words would
sound like:
> *YOU'RE GAY.*

He felt he owed the other gays answers, a detailed explanation,
beginning with his teenage years, of how he had come to be in
this relationship, of how his story was not the same as histories
of gay men lying to their families and taking their wedding rings
off before going to the baths. But at some point, he began to
worry that his detailed explanations came across as
> defensive,

so he said very little about his relationship
which suggested
> he had something to hide,

or rather,
> he was hiding

which meant
> GAY.

Until the word *queer* found him. The word had been surfacing
more often in his social circle—mentions of *queer* parties or
*queer* art—but he hadn't immediately considered it as his own.

He recognized that she and he could hold hands and kiss in most spaces and that landlords wouldn't think twice about renting to them. But *queer* spoke to all the other spaces and moments his body and his heart didn't fit into. *Queer* acknowledged both the cocksucking porn on his laptop and the wanting to be underneath her. *Queer* encompassed every time his gender was read as wrong and the words "fucking faggot" were spat at him. Wearing *queer* allowed him to shed the sense that he was lying to one group or another. His love, and the person he cherished most, no longer needed to be kept secret. He could be everything all at once. Ironically, *queer* meant whole.

*So I have been thinking of identifying as queer,* he said to her.

*Well, I love my queer partner,* she responded. Hearing her say those words, he realized that she too needed the word *queer*, especially in that sentence, if only to be able to counter the Duped Victim narrative that had been projected onto her.

His claiming of queer did not suffice for the gays. If anything, it only angered them.

## SCENE FOUR
*(Setting: Holiday party—group of friends sitting around fireplace in living room)*

Him: *Actually, my partner is a woman…*
Stranger 2: *You fuck a woman?*
Him: *Yes?*
Stranger 2: *Really? But you are the GAYEST man I have ever met!*

## SCENE FIVE

*(Setting: Starbucks—he and Friend 2 are having a heated conversation)*

Him: *Well, that's why I prefer* queer *as a label.*
Friend 2: *But you know you can't really call yourself queer without a dick in your mouth.*

It occurred to him that the gays and the straights had more in common than he had considered before. Just like the straights, the gays were intent on preserving and presenting a uniform, singular version of themselves; in this case, their gayness. They hadn't been saying: *you're gay! You're GAY!* They were actually saying: *Our way! OUR way!*

• • •

Sunday mornings on the balcony. Fresh croissants, Havarti, and sparkling grape juice. Her slicing the Havarti so thin that it tasted like a perfect layer of butter.

Applying her rose-tinted lip gloss to his lips with her fingers. Lip-glossed kissing. *So sticky*, he said.

Slow dancing under the first snowfall outside their apartment on Bloor Street, her nose pressed into his cheek for warmth. Slow dancing while waiting for the Queen streetcar and him being grateful that the streetcar was late, as usual. Trying to slow dance in the shower, and her getting shampoo in her eyes. Slow dancing while brushing their teeth before bed to Madonna's "Crazy for You." *Two by two, their bodies become one.*

Waiting for his workday to be over, to be standing outside their apartment, keys already in his hand, hoping she would be on the other side. Waiting to flood her face with kisses and then share the newest work or friend or family gossip. Waiting for Thursday night to see the midnight premiere screening of *Harry Potter and the Order of the Phoenix*. Waiting for the summer, for evening walks and gelato and her body glowing with a light sheen of sweat. Waiting for her thirtieth birthday to surprise her with a trip to New York City.

Arguing about her lack of effort with his friends as they walked up to the Eiffel Tower. Preparing for his job interview on the road trip to Ottawa. *You will be charming, you always are,* she said. Sweeping up her long curly hair from every corner of their apartment and missing that hair when she was out of town for weeks. Surprising her at Pearson Airport when she returned.

A *Felicity* marathon during the February snowstorm, and getting sick from eating too much stale delivery pizza. Splurging on a clear glass punch bowl for their Thanksgiving dinners, her favourite holiday. Fingering her on the Ossington bus on their way to his friend Trisha's housewarming, and her being sure that they were going to get kicked off. Trying on her black lingerie after making her promise not to take any photos.

Days of him disappearing into inexplicable sadness, and she his beacon. Holding her hand so tightly at the hospital while they watched her grandmother die. Him wanting her to know that however great her loss, he was beside her if she needed to lean.

Two a.m. in bed, belting out a medley from Tegan and Sara's *So Jealous*, her impressing him by mimicking the intricate background vocal parts. His snoring keeping her awake for hours. Her holding onto his body after his alarm clock beeped, strategically rolling her leg over his. Her saying, *One more minute.* Every morning.

This is how seven years goes by.

• • •

KALI

I have never understood the relentless desire for immortality, which would suggest a cosmic irony, since I am Parvati, Embodiment of Life. But there is a reason why my partner is The Destroyer—I understand the necessity of balance, that the beauty of life is truly in its precariousness, its limitation. The beauty of life is that it ends. If I were mortal and could be granted anything, I assure you, my request would not be for something as dull as longevity.

Centuries ago, the evil demon Mahishasura prayed for so long, forsaking food and water, that his prayers began to generate heat, a heat that could turn toxic and would need to be tempered. Brahma, the Father of Men, appeared above him.

*Oh Mahishasura! I have heard your prayers and bless you. What do you desire?*

*Lord Brahma! I desire to live forever.*

*Son, this cannot be granted to any man. Ask again.*

*Then make me indestructible by any god…*

This boon gave Mahishasura permission to express his brutality, which he did, knowing that there could be no divine retribution. It is tragic how many equate this kind of power with being a god.

The gods gathered at Vaikunta to seek counsel and comfort from the Great Protector, Narayana. It was eventually determined that gender was a loophole, and I could slip through it. I am not a god, after all, but a goddess.

On the battlefield, I took on a new warrior form as Durga. Eight different weapons in eight different arms. My lion attacked Mahishasura effortlessly, and I stabbed my trishul into his gut. A clean, swift victory. The gods sighed.

Until the first drop of his blood hit the earth. The red vibrated and exploded into another version of Mahishasura. *Alive.*

How could this be? I pounced on the new Mahishasura, this time slicing off his arms and legs. More blood was spilled. More versions of him sprang forth surrounding me from every direction, every one of him laughing at a secret joke that I was not prepared for.

I retreated into the cave of my mind, while Durga continued to fight valiantly.

*Who bestowed this power upon him?*

*Who would dare to betray me like this?*

The questions circulated and repeated, new questions forming after every cycle. One new question for every new Mahishasura.

*How can there be life without my will, my touch, my love?*

*How can there be life born from death?*

I began to lose sight of my own body and the battlefield under a thick haze of red. I was drowning.

MahishasuraMahishasuraMahishasuraMahishasuraMahishasur aMahishasuraMahishasuraMahishasuraMahishasuraMahisha suraMahishasuraMahishasuraMahishasuraMahishasuMahisha suraMahishasuraMahishasuraMahishasuraMahishasuraMahi shasuraMahishas—

For the first time, I wanted to die. Not out of fear or hopelessness but to understand my enemy. To understand the dark magic behind the mystery I couldn't solve, the multiplication I couldn't divide. Perhaps death was the only way to know the other side of the equation.

That desire expanded and burst out of my head, in the shape of *her*. For a moment, I thought it was Shiv. The long, unruly hair, the hunger for death in her eyes.

I watched this being who had erupted from my brow get on her knees, open her mouth, and drink the red river that surrounded us. With every drop of blood, she became more excited, her black skin more radiant. At one point she looked up at me, smiling with all her teeth exposed, her red tongue dangling, and I understood that she hadn't manifested to kill. It was pleasure she sought, the sweet savour of life.

It was at that moment that I recognized her as myself.

*Kali*, I whispered.

She winked and said, without moving her lips:

*The beauty of life is the will to live.*

How could I have missed that? I had been caught by the wrong questions. The *who*s or *how*s didn't matter. The *why*, however, the *why* was crucial. *Why* was Mahishasura replicating? Because that is precisely what life was engineered to do—it fights to sustain itself, to survive, despite its limitations. He was simply acting in accordance with his very nature, under my law.

Once I remembered this, I was able to kill him.

• • •

*How did you get inside your body?*

*How did I get inside my body?* she repeated, checking to see if she had heard him correctly, running her fingers through his hair, his head on her lap.

*Yes…*

He could never escape the jarring feeling that he and his body were still two separate entities with two separate operating systems. Maneuvering his body felt like driving with the emergency brake on, the low and constant growl of dragging a frame embedded with an unforgotten history of hate. He wished that he believed he would be better suited for a different body, but another body represented only another confinement, another set of parameters. What he craved was the kind of repair that would unite driver and car as one, make them synchronous. He wondered if this was even possible, or if everyone silently struggled with this duality.

*What do you mean?*

*The only time I feel inside my body is when it is next to yours. Like right now.*

• • •

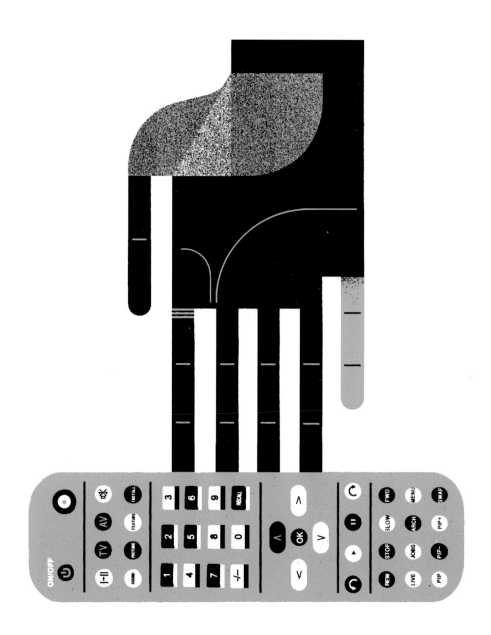

Next to her body, he had grown into his own body in ways he hadn't thought possible after high school, revelling in its colour and even deriving pleasure from it. Next to her body, he felt a seamless, integrated connection to his own. Next to her body, he felt hope.

But in her absence, when she travelled to Montreal for work or to Edmonton to visit her family, the weight of his body would always reappear. Over the years, and the longer she was gone, the more the weight would grow, like a monstrous exaggeration of itself.

The changes were small at first. He was procrastinating doing the day's errands, lounging on the couch, the first time he imagined his right hand had grown another finger. He tried to shake it off.

*I don't like myself when I am not with her,* he mumbled to the finger, thinking aloud.

He spent the weekend trying his best to ignore it, but whenever he used his hand to reach for a glass or put on his jacket, and he was forced to look at it, he felt a nauseating disappointment with himself, as though the finger was a manifestation of all his flaws and inadequacies.

*I shouldn't have slept in. I should have gone for a run this morning. I should have worked harder at the office this week. I should have bought groceries. I don't read enough. I don't call my parents enough. I am a bad son. I am a bad friend. I am not good enough. I am not good enough. I am not good enough. I am not good enough.*

As soon as she was home again, the new finger vanished before he could even show it to her and he forgot about it altogether.

During her subsequent travels, his body grew a third arm, and a fourth, and a second tongue and even a tail. He could never predict where a new growth might spring out. He would turn off all the lights in their apartment to avoid seeing himself and wait for her in darkness. Sometimes he would whisper to himself: *Take a knife to it.* The thought wasn't rooted in a desire to inflict pain, but rather in the reasoning that if he cut off the part, perhaps he could study it inside out and understand it and himself better.

Just like the finger, these extra limbs would all fade when she returned, when she merely smiled at him or caressed his face with the back of her hand.

*How did you do that?* he asked each time.

*Do what?*

He didn't respond because he didn't know how to ask: *How did you make me myself again? How did you make the beast disappear?*

He began to sleep at the edge of their bed, resentful of her presence, of her body that seemed to know his body better than he did, and his new growths took longer to shed. He had more and more difficulty knowing which body was real, and some days, he even believed his imagined body was his true body, forcing him to bail out of social commitments and repeatedly call in sick at work.

*I am a bad worker. I am a bad friend. I disappoint everyone. I can't be what they want. Everyone is better off without me. I am not good enough. I am not good enough. I am not good enough. I am not good enough. I am not enough. I am not enough. I am not enough. I am not enough.*

• • •

After we killed him, I lost her.

Kali had lapped up every drop of his blood, preventing new Mahishasuras from sprouting, and I steadfastly slaughtered the remaining Mahishasuras. Together we were a terrifying and magnificent team. But then, high on the taste of life, she began feeding on any human in sight, dancing feverishly as she drank their innocent bodies dry, her eyes rolling in circles. She wanted more.

*Kali!* I said, over and over again, trying to awaken her from her madness. She was beyond my reach. For a moment, I wanted her to have everything. Why must we always prioritize harmony and consider consequence? What lessons do we miss by suppressing rage and chaos? Why did Shiv alone have domain over destruction?

These thoughts only heightened Kali's delirium, and she nodded violently in agreement. I could taste the blood in her mouth. It was sour and cold, like rotting plants, foretelling the extinction ahead. *No,* I whispered, shifting my attention to the humans, moving as many as I could to safety.

*Into the trees! Hurry!* I yelled.

Suddenly, Shiv appeared. He looked at me, then at her, and then at me again. Although he had never seen Kali before, he recognized her as part of me. He approached her from behind, waited for her to be mid-air, and stealthily laid himself down beneath her feet.

*Shiv! What are you doing? She will crush you!* I cried.

Kali danced on his body, oblivious to him, her feet pounding on his chest and her arms flailing in every direction. Shiv's eyes were closed. I knew that I had to push her off of him somehow, even if this meant incurring her wrath. Before I had the chance, she wobbled and look down, startled.

*Blue, I remember you*, she said. She disappeared back into my brow, leaving a smell of smoke, of fires quenched.

I rushed to Shiv's side.

*Shiv, I am so sorry. She was insatiable. I should have...*

He opened his eyes and smiled.

*You should have everything*, he said, echoing my earlier thought.

*But I do!*

Perhaps the only way to steady her—and me—was for him to rest his body under hers.

• • •

*Can't you see what is happening to me?* he said, massaging his temples with vigour, trying to pacify the throbbing under his forehead.

She had not mentioned anything about his new body, but he assumed she was being kind, the way she would pretend not to see the bulbous zit on his face, even when he pointed it out.

*Yes, you seem different,* she said.

*So you can see my new leg?*

*A new leg? No… you seem restless. And unhapp—*

*What about my tail?* he interrupted and pointed behind him.

She examined him closely.

*I still don't see anything, love. You are as beautiful as ever.*

He cringed. Why couldn't she see what he saw?

*Just be honest. Please. I need you to be honest.*

She walked towards him and said, *You are beautiful.*

Whenever she looked at him, including at this moment, her entire face turned to light. He wondered what it would feel like to look at himself and see what she saw, to shine as she did, or at least feel a lightness in his body. He imagined what it would be

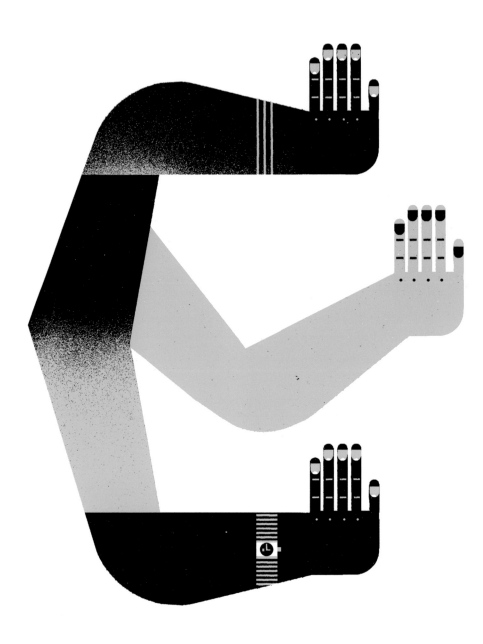

like to walk down the street, a tower of light, fully connected to his limbs and senses.

His three arms pushed her away, refusing to succumb to her light, and he grew silent.

*Please just talk to me.*

One of his tongues held the other tongue down.

*Listen, I love you. Whatever is going on, we can figure this out together.*

His top tongue loosened.

*What did you just say?* he asked.

*I said I love you.*

His new leg dissolved.

*Can you say it again?*

*I love you…*

In minutes, his body was entirely restored.

• • •

He found himself looking forward to her next departure, feeling a new confidence as a result of the secret he had uncovered.

When she did leave, and a second head appeared on his shoulder, he tried to conjure her love. *She loves you, she loves you, she loves you,* he said to the head. It refused to disappear.

*Why isn't this working? She loves you, she loves you, she loves you,* his original head kept telling the other, his voice increasing in volume, thinking perhaps the new head's ears could not hear very well.

*You're wasting your breath,* the new head replied. And it was right. Her love did seem to have limitations. Its effects were temporary, and he desired a more permanent solution.

*But she loves you,* he cried. *She loves you, she loves you … I love you,* he accidentally blurted.

*No, you don't,* the other head responded. It was right again.

He was about to surrender when he recalled a memory. They were on her bedroom floor, her body arched into his, and his face buried in her hair. His index finger moved slowly but deliberately along her bare back, spelling words, which he punctuated with a kiss. This was how he had told her he loved her, the very first time.

Why had he never thought to apply the same ardour to his own body? What would happen if he did?

He said the words again, this time earnestly, as if it were a prayer:

*I*
*love*
*you.*

The head vanished. His body quivered with an unfamiliar sense of victory. He closed his eyes.

• • •

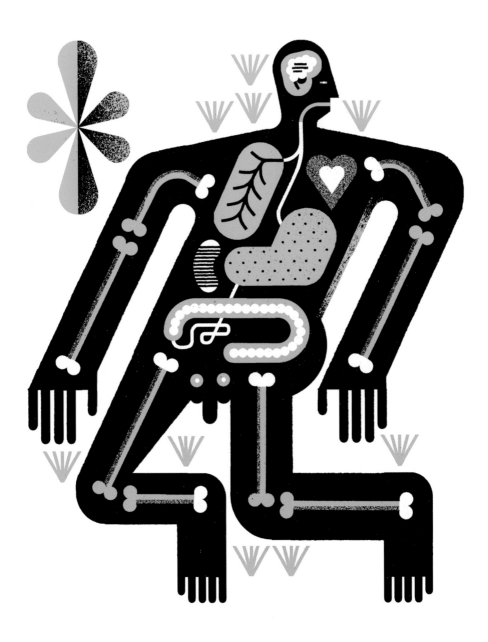

He pictured himself running in an open field. With every thrust forward and every leap, he felt boundless, reaching higher and higher until he soared right out of his body as a light blue glow. *At last!* he exclaimed, suspended in air.

Language dissipated.

Words and flesh were replaced by absolute feeling, a feeling he had experienced only in brief bursts—the grand heat pulsing beneath laughter, a flashback of a treasured moment, or every time his hairs stood on end. In this pure state, it was impossible for him to perceive any error in or damage to himself.

He basked.

Time drifted.

Until something below caught his attention. Illuminated by starlight, his body appeared translucent on the emerald green grass. Astounded by the sight of it, the sturdiness of its structure, he wasn't certain at first that it was even his own. With no mirror or person to reflect himself back to him, he studied his body with curiosity. He noted the callouses on the soles of his feet, the contracting and relaxing of his diaphragm, the blood circulating through his maze of arteries, the protection of his eyelids, and the intricacy of his brain. He twinkled in awe, humbled by his body, which seemed to continuously labour for him, without recognition. Could it be that all this time he and his body were actually teammates, were partners?

He opened his eyes and wrapped his arms around himself.

• • •

*I don't like myself when I am not with you.* He finally said the words to her. *And I want to.*

◆ ◆ ◆

# GANESHA

*Pita, can I talk to you about something?*

*Anything, son.*

*Sometimes when I close my eyes, I see… a forest.*

*A forest? Do you see anything else?*

*No. Just a forest.*

Shiv looks at me. I look away for a moment and then nod quietly. He nods back. We had known from *that* day that *this* day was unavoidable.

*Come with me, Ganesh.*

Although I am not explicitly invited, I join them.

On Shiv's bull, Nandi, we travel west of the mountains in silence. In a few months, these parts will be submerged under snow. But for now and for the last time this year, the leaves are showing off their colour—every shade of red, orange, and yellow. I can feel my own colour fade as we approach our destination. I want to say to our son:

*I failed you. I should have protected you.*

Instead, I hear his voice. *Pita! That is it. That is the place I see.* Ganesh points ahead.

*I know…*

*How do you know?*

*Because. This is where your head is from.*

*My head?*

*Yes. Haven't you wondered why you have the head of an elephant?*

*I have not… Uma has always said that I am special.*

*You are. You are.*

Shiv closes his eyes, bows his head, and then begins the tale of how he cut off Ganesh's head. He tells the story with as much detail as he can summon as penance.

I want to hold his hand. I want to hold Ganesh's hand. I want to place their hands in each other's.

I study Ganesh's face. It is calm and unshaken, with no lines of doubt on his forehead, his eyes clear and gleaming. It is hard for me to imagine that once he had a different face, that once this face, this face I love, belonged to a demon.

*What happened to my other head?* is Ganesh's first question after Shiv finishes, reading my mind.

*We buried it,* Shiv says.

*Where?*

*Here, actually. Under the tallest tree. Parvati, your Uma, insisted that since we had taken something from the forest, something had to be returned.*

*Please take me to it.*

Shiv guides us solemnly through the trees that sway around us until we reach it. I recall the tree by the colour of its bark, a hint of maroon, though it is no longer the tallest of its companions.

*This is it.*

Ganesh bends down and puts his head to the fallen leaves and wet earth.

Then he begins to sing. I immediately recognize his song—the notes too high, the melody too beautiful.

I stand over him and sing with him.

• • •

Home is a painting. A painting purchased from IKEA.

*Do you think it's in bad taste? IKEA art?*

*Who cares? It's beautiful.*

It was.

It was a painting of Manhattan in black and white and from the sky's perspective. All the grandeur and busyness of a big city captured and unusually still.

They had hung the painting over their bed. On some mornings, after he would leave for work, she would linger under the duvet, look up, and reminisce about their travel adventures. And whenever he was distracted while he read, he would stare at it to ground him. He dreamed names and lives and quests associated with each apartment light. He even reserved a small window light in the right-hand corner just for them.

*Wouldn't it be great to live in New York for a year?* she had said.

*It would.*

*We could really experience the city. Not just as tourists.*

*Yeah, but there is no way they are going to let two brown people move to New York.*

*Especially not with your beard.*

They chuckled.

The painting became a fixture of their bedroom, as vital as the bed itself, and over time, he couldn't imagine their home without it.

Now, they had the unimaginable task of drawing a line between their possessions, to be divided into her boxes and his boxes. As his hand touched every object and fixture, it re-awakened a unique memory, a precious history that was embedded in each.

one painting
one bed
one TV
one couch
one recliner
four bar stools
four mugs
eight plates
four bowls
two frying pans
one bottle of ketchup
one bottle of soy sauce
one bottle of Patak's pickle
one box of pasta
two towels
two dish towels
one bottle of Windex
two sets of bed sheets
one clotheshorse

one stool

two lamps

two bookshelves

one alarm clock

one desk

one cutlery set

He was certain his heart would literally break and often crossed his arms over his chest to keep it intact. But he was profoundly wrong. He discovered that a home could break, but a heart could not. That their home could break, but his heart would not despite how much he wished it would. His heart could actually withstand the dissolution of his home, and this was where the pain came from. Pain was his heart bearing and bearing and bearing and bearing and bearing and bearing and bearing and bearing. Pain was the sound of his relentless heartbeat, pushing forward as though nothing was changing. Pain was knowing that he was the cause of her pain, the reason why her eyes were without their sparkle and wonder. Pain was not knowing if he was making a monumental mistake, wanting to reach out to her and say, *I'm sorry, I've changed my mind.*

Pain was a bare white wall where a painting once hung. A painting sold to strangers through Craigslist.

• • •

After he left her, he turned to another body—water.

Every day, the water taught him something new about how to connect to his own body.

The first step, the hardest step, was taking off his clothes. Allowing his body to be exposed to light and air—to be free. Only then could he enter the pool.

His second challenge was learning how to float. He tread close to the pool's edge in case he needed to latch onto it for support. His body fought hard against the water, resisting it, not unlike how he had resisted his own body. It was only after he exhausted himself from splashing and kicking aimlessly, when he fully surrendered to the water, that he stopped drowning.

As his body elongated with each lap, the water encouraged him to stretch out and slow down his thoughts so he could observe each one. The buzzing of his never-ending to-do list softened and lost its urgency.

*Respond to email.*

*R e s p o n d t o e m a*

*R e s p o n d t o e*

*R e s p o n d t o*

*R e s p o n d*

The water showed him how to release the day's disappointments with each breath in-between strokes, so that the weight he carried was only that of his physical self. When his head was fully submerged again, the taste of chlorine acted as the final cleanse. Drained of the superfluous, his body didn't feel so unmanageable.

The water also gave him an open and quiet space where he could cry without being seen. Water to water—this is when he felt they were closest, they were friends.

He often thought of her when he was in the water. Although a chapter of their relationship had ended, one year later, he found that there was still no period to their sentence. Their sentence kept finding a way, because they kept finding a way to make room for a comma and another comma and another conjunction, because there was still so much to share, still so much more to say.

• • •

*Once we were bacteria. We were simple cells for three billion years.*

*We grew complex. Our cells wanted to grow, work, and reproduce.*

*Once we were jellyfish, free-swimming.*

*We learned how to crawl before we grew feet. We colonized the land. Our blood turned warm. Our arms stretched into wings, and we sought homes everywhere beneath the clouds.*

*Because it was necessary.*

*For millennia, I have been evolving into this version of myself, this body. To know yours.*

*Because it was necessary.*

## ACKNOWLEDGMENTS

This book would not be possible without Shemeena Shraya, Trish Yeo, and Raymond Biesinger.

A special thank you to the Arsenal Pulp Press team, Adam Holman, Farzana Doctor, Karen Campos, Maureen Hynes, Margot Francis, Caleb Nault, Marilyn McLean, Amber Dawn, Kathryn Payne, Tegan Quin, Sara Quin, RM Vaughn, Shyam Selvadurai, Rakesh Satyal, Dale Hall, Katherine Friesen, and my family.

**VIVEK SHRAYA** is a multimedia artist, working in the mediums of music, performance, literature, and film. His first book, *God Loves Hair*, was a Lambda Literary Award finalist first published in 2011 and reissued in a new edition from Arsenal Pulp Press in 2014. Winner of the We Are Listening International Singer/Songwriter Award, Vivek has released albums ranging from acoustic folk-rock to electro synth-pop. His most recent is *Breathe Again*, a tribute to the songs of R&B artist Babyface. His short film, *What I LOVE about being QUEER*, has expanded to include an online project and Lambda Literary Award-nominated book with contributions from around the world. He lives in Toronto.

**RAYMOND BIESINGER** is a self-taught illustrator based in Montreal who spent a very long time in Canada's west. His work has appeared in everything from *The New Yorker* to *Le Monde* to *The Walrus* to *Dwell*, and he likes concepts, making music, progressive politics, and a curious mix of minimalism and maximalism. He deploys physical things, electronic means, and a BA in history to make his images, and has done so in over 1,400 projects since the year 2000.

DA    06/15